Dragons
ARE PEOPLE, TOO

SARAH NICOLAS

Entangled Publishing, LLC
2614 South Timberline Road
Suite 109
Fort Collins, CO 80525
Visit our website at www.entangledpublishing.com.

Entangled Teen is an imprint of Entangled Publishing, LLC.

Edited by Kate Brauning
Cover design by Kelley York
Cover art by Shutterstock

Manufactured in the United States of America

First Edition April 2015

For my grandma,
who gave me my love of reading.

Chapter One

Well, crap. Mission Intelligence got it wrong. Again.

I mean, seriously? Heat sensors? When your operatives have a core body temperature of 142 degrees, that should be the first thing you check for. Deep breaths, Kitty. I daydream about ripping Simon a new one as I scale up the three stories of crumbling stone.

So now I cling to the east wall of the Lebanese embassy in D.C. with a diplomatic document pouch hanging from my belt.

I'm overly conscious of the two security cameras aimed at my back, despite the full-body black catsuit with matching ski mask that Draconic Intelligence Command (or, as I like to call it, DIC) requires me to wear. Sirens blare, telling me security already knows we're here, but I still can't let them see my face. And, more importantly, I can't let them see me change.

Beside me, Wallace scrabbles, then loses his balance and

falls twenty feet to the ground, hitting the wall at least twice in the process. Rookie. His breath comes fast, but he's uninjured. He could probably fall from three times that height without a scratch.

"Kitty." Even his whisper has a British accent. He lies sprawled on the immaculate walled lawn of the Embassy and slowly makes his way to his feet. "I can't make it without changing."

"No!" I yell, then catch myself and lower my voice to something more like a hiss. "Absolutely not. Do you have any idea how many cameras are on you right now? You can make it."

His hooded head flicks toward the cameras mounted around the lawn and back to me. I can't see his face through the black cloth, but something in his body language betrays his panic. I may be only sixteen, but this is Wallace's first mission, and I have been training since I was four. Though he's thirteen years older than me, I am the senior field agent; I have to get him through this. Thank the Gods it's not his dragon half that's panicking, just the human half. It's bad, but it's at least manageable. And, you know, not catastrophic.

I soften my voice and mimic the tone my mother uses when she convinces me to do something I don't want to do. "I'm almost to the top. I'll lower a rope when I get there, okay?"

His head snaps up and down in something resembling agreement. I almost feel sorry for him. We'd all told him his first mission would be a piece of cake. It should've been, anyway, if it wasn't for those freaking heat sensors.

It doesn't help that English dragons aren't exactly the ideal operatives for a stealth mission. They are too big, less agile than Chinese or African dragons, and they don't like any situation they can't bully their way out of. But if you need fire power or brute strength, they're definitely the dragons for you. During normal operations, this mission should've been given to an African dragon, but Command always wants every operative to train in every kind of mission.

Even if, like Wallace, they'll probably never see the same situation again.

I'm about five feet below the roof ledge when I hear the dogs barking. The first sleek shape rounds the corner from the north wall at a full sprint, his claws scrabbling in the lawn as he slides around the turn. A second set of snapping, snarling jaws follows close behind and I know their human counterparts can't be too far away—probably with something a little more dangerous than a mouth full of razor-sharp teeth.

In the next instant, I realize Wallace's chest is heaving too quickly, his eyes rolling frantically in their sockets. A panicking rookie means my night is about to get so much worse. The fact that it's not his dragon half raging out of control is now about as comforting as a single ice cube when you're on fire.

"No!" I scream, not caring about being heard now. "Wallace! Don't! That's an order."

He's going to break the Number One rule of an operative for the Draconic Intelligence Command: Don't let *anyone* know what you are. At any one time, there are maybe six or seven humans who know about our kind for assorted reasons. But there has never been any actual evidence.

But that all changes the moment his green and purple patterned wings snap out of his back, his body following closely behind, his clothes dematerializing.

Crap. Crap. Crap.

Before the dogs even make it halfway across the lawn, he becomes a twenty-foot monstrosity of muscle and scales. Because they're the showy ones, English dragons are the ones always depicted in movies: a four-legged dinosaur-like body, a bearded head with jewel-bright eyes, a long tail ending in an arrow-shaped tip, and massive leathery wings. His ebony talons dig deep gouges into the soft soil of the Embassy's lawn.

The dogs stop and paw at the ground, shaking their heads in confusion. Their prey has suddenly become a predator. A powerful wind swirls around the lawn with the first beat of Wallace's wings and it almost knocks me off my perch on the Embassy's wall. The dogs whimper and sprint for the useless cover of the nearest bush. Wallace aims a spurt of fire at each of the security cameras, leaving behind charred metal poles and the toxic smell of burned plastic. Like that will do any good now.

Before I decide what to do next, his tail wraps around my waist—with the sharp defensive scales pointed *away* from my body—and we rise above the Embassy. I swoop up and over his back and he lets go, depositing me roughly on his neck in front of his wings. He climbs high into the clouds and heads toward Draconic Intelligence Command. My mind races, trying to figure out if I can get into the Embassy and destroy the security tapes before an army descends on me. I abandon that plan as soon as I remember Simon explaining how Embassy security footage is uploaded to an off-site server in real time. If the Lebanese release those tapes—I can't even imagine what will happen.

As soon as we are inside a thick cloud, I jump off his

back and shift into my dragon shape in mid-air, wanting to distance myself at least symbolically from his actions before we reach DIC. Chinese dragons don't have wings, but we manipulate the earth's magnetic fields in order to fly. My dragon body is much longer and thinner than Wallace's, with a shape more like a thirty-foot green serpent with four feet and yellow spines all the way down my back. I also have this crazy red, green, and purple comb on top of my head that looks like some punk kid stuck his finger in a light socket. As soon as I shift, psychic waves of fear and regret pouring from Wallace pound against my consciousness and nearly knock me out of the sky. He's got enough of his own to deal with, so I guard my panic from him as best I can. If I'm being honest, I fly a little slower than top speed toward DIC and Wallace follows my lead, neither of us wanting to explain what just took place to my Draco Team Delta leader—who also happens to be my mom. I've messed up a lot before. Like, *a lot.* But I have never been this deep in crap.

As the humans would say, this is a game changer. If those tapes get out, this will go down in the history books as the most significant event in dragonkind history. And there, in black Helvetica on semi-gloss paper, will be the name of the person in charge when everything went to hell.

• • •

"Katherine Lung."

I wince as my full first name bounces around the stark gray walls and I press my palms against the cool fiberglass table in front of me. My mother hasn't used my first name since I was twelve and I decided to sneak into a mission briefing. I had just developed the ability to turn myself invisible and thought myself invincible also. The game ended when I touched Draco Team Beta Commander's arm and he disappeared from everyone else's view. I hadn't realized my power would turn any dragon I touched invisible too—and then he could see me. As a dragon, I was too big to escape from the conference room, so I'd had to shift to human form, which meant dropping the cloaking shields.

Today is so much worse.

Mom shakes her head and her eyes give me the I'm-so-disappointed-in-you glare all Chinese mothers master as soon as they give birth. I would prefer any amount of shouting or even physical punishment over this stare. Make me run sprints until I throw up or spar until my hands bleed—as long as I don't have to see how disappointed my mom is in me.

All the team commanders and the director had listened to the story Wallace and I told, then immediately darted out of the room to begin the attempts at damage control.

Now, my mom and I sit alone in the mission briefing room. The dim lighting in here almost lets the red streak in her hair blend in to the gentle sweep of her sable French twist, and it definitely softens the wrinkles just starting to pop up around her eyes.

I can't take the silence and the staring; I have to say something. That's probably her plan.

"Technically," I hedge, "I didn't do anything wrong."

It would probably sound more convincing if I believed it.

"You were the senior agent," she says, cool and calm. "You are responsible for the actions of your team." She's legendary for her repose in the worst of situations, even when in dragon form. Most people mistake it for serenity, but I know her secret truth: control is the only way she feels powerful. When she can't control everything around her, the only thing left is her emotions.

And all that emotional control my mother has? She must have taken mine too, because I'm utterly lacking.

"We shouldn't have even been on the side of the building. The heat sensors—"

She cuts me off by standing up straight and crossing her arms over her chest. For a five-foot-nothing middle-aged Asian woman, my mom can be intimidating as hell. The power and majesty of the dragons seems to roll off her in waves stronger than any other dragon I've ever met. Her eyes say what she doesn't have to: No Excuses.

"Do you have any idea what this could mean?" she asks. I open my mouth to respond, but she obviously doesn't want an answer. "Depending on what the Lebanese government decides to do with the security footage, this could be the end of life as we know it."

Before tonight, I've always accepted the old party line that a dragon had never been caught on film. But just now, in this room, it doesn't seem possible. Between security cameras, tourists with digital cameras around their necks, and the ever-present cell phone camera, I can't figure out how we've gone so long without something like this happening. Impossible.

Obviously.

I realize my mom's glaring at me again, waiting for some kind of response. The air in my chest feels combustible, pressing against my ribs until I'm afraid I might burst.

Finally, I let it all out with one violent exhalation. My palms slap the table, startling both of us.

"I don't know what you want me to say, Mom. He panicked." I feel my voice waver and I clench my fists, willing my body to at least pretend I'm not scared out of my mind. "There was nothing I could've done. He wasn't ready; he shouldn't have been there."

As soon as the words form on my tongue, before they even cross my lips, I know I shouldn't say this. Sending Wallace on his first mission was my mom's decision. And I question it? Gods, having your mom as your commanding officer really sucks sometimes.

They say Chinese dragons don't have anything to do with fire, but I would bet every one of the very few things I own that I see flames flicker in my mom's eyes just now.

"He was more than ready; he's been training for a full year." She swallows, dousing the flames in her eyes with great effort. "Perhaps it was his commanding officer who wasn't ready."

Anger bursts in my chest and drives me to stand up, towering a whole four inches over my mom. "Know what? I think you're right. I'm freaking sixteen years old. This whole DIC thing—"

"D-I-C," my mom interrupts, correcting my pronunciation. "How many times do I have to tell you to drop the childish nickname for our employer?"

I roll my eyes. "My point is: I should be going to high school dances and studying for my biology test, not running missions to steal diplomatic papers for the U.S. government."

Truth be told, I love working for DIC. And I actually do go to high school, but only because I happen to be the same age as the president's son. I can take out any assailant as well as three grown men with guns and I don't stand out at a high school like the other Secret Service agents. Or, at least, I don't stand out in the same way. Our family has been serving presidents since Woodrow Wilson, so a background check isn't even necessary. The U.S. government *is* my background.

But I'm not entirely ready to be treated like a full-blown adult, either. I'm just wise enough to realize I'm still a teenager, caught halfway between kid and adult. Sometimes, I need my mom to be just my mom. And being semi-responsible for both an international incident and the exposure of an entire species that thrives on secrecy? This could be one of those times.

"Well, you might soon get your wish," Mom says. "That is, as long as the public doesn't find out what you are."

I try to stop what happens next, I truly do. But my chest tightens, and my eyes sting, begging for a release. Dragons don't cry like humans do. Our bodies are too hot to let liquid water hang around for very long, but even though we don't have actual tears to shed, the rest of the crying is the same. The aching in the chest, the irregular breathing, the red puffy eyes—all unfortunate side effects of our human inclination. I've always wondered if dragons had to put up with this a hundred thousand years ago, before we developed our human forms. Might be worth it, trading my opposable thumbs for never having to cry again. But then I imagine always being able to feel everyone's emotions and I'm back in the humanoid camp again.

I don't think my mom realizes what is happening to me at first, but when I cover my face with my hands and a loud, embarrassing sob escapes my throat, she rushes to my side of the table and wraps her thin, iron arms around my shaking shoulders. My mom may be one tough-as-dragon-teeth commander, but she's also a good mother. She usually knows when to bark out orders and when to hand out hugs.

"I'm sorry, Kitty," she says, after letting me cry myself out. "You're one of my most reliable operatives. Sometimes I forget you're just a kid."

Normally, I would object to the last part, but right now, when I just quite possibly ruined *everything*? I need to be "just a kid."

Chapter Two

The absolute last thing I want to do four hours after the meeting with my mom is wake up to my regular alarm and get ready for school. My fingers itch to pick up the little clock and throw it across the meager length of my barracks. Even though my entire world may or may not have been altered last night, I have an obligation to Jacob, the president's son.

The beige walls of my windowless room do nothing to encourage me out of bed. Nor does the thought of sitting through lectures on subjects I mastered years ago.

I shower in the tiny stall that gives me just enough room to turn around. The water is still vaporizing from my skin when I slip on one of my more comfortable purple dresses made of organic cotton. The dress allows for a wider range of motion than jeans and it's the same shade as the purple streaks in my chin-length, stick-straight black hair. I'm not exactly the kind of girl who spends hours fixing her hair and putting on makeup, so I'm ready about twelve minutes after waking up. Just before I grab my backpack, a knock sounds at the door.

Like every other DIC operative, I live in barracks at the underground complex so, usually, a knock at my door means a last-minute mission. Adrenaline starts pumping, waking me up faster than the cup of coffee I had planned on grabbing from the cafeteria. I open the door to find Wallace, looking like he hasn't slept for weeks, standing there. The workout clothes he's wearing look like they were plucked from a dirty hamper fifteen seconds ago.

"Director wants to see us," he says. His voice sounds broken.

Crap. This can't be any flavor of good.

I nod and follow him silently through the familiar maze of windowless, colorless hallways to the director's office. Beside me, Wallace shifts his shoulders incessantly. I can tell he's upset, but I'm not sure what brand of upset this is. Nervousness? Remorse? It's so much easier when we're both dragons and I can simply know what he's feeling as accurately as I know what color an apple is. I'm not really the comforting type, but it's driving me nuts, so I raise a hand and place it on his shoulder, patting lightly. Am I doing this right? I don't know if it's the soldier in me or the dragon, but sympathy isn't part of my skill set.

He turns his head just an inch to smile at me, but it's one of those smiles people give you when they want to say, "I appreciate the sentiment, but it doesn't really make me feel better." Poor guy. He's not really cut out for this. Who would ever guess the Clark Kent to an English dragon's Superman would be the biggest computer nerd I've ever met? He's only here because the CIA caught him hacking into their system. Well, they caught him the fourth time around. When they found out he was a dragon, he had a pretty easy choice to make: interminable solitary confinement in an undisclosed secret prison or join DIC, keeping both his fortune and his relative freedom.

"You know everyone else is calling me Number One?" he says.

Because he broke the Number One rule. I stifle a laugh and he definitely notices. "Word spreads fast," is all I can offer for comfort. "What are they calling me?"

"Unlucky," he says. "Because you got stuck with me."

Ouch.

Marcy, the director's assistant, is busying herself at her desk by shuffling and reshuffling the same stack of paper. She smiles warmly at me, but intense worry swims in her eyes. Marcy is an English dragon who no longer goes out on missions despite being only thirty-something years old. She suffered a brain injury four years ago that keeps her from fully changing back to her human form; shimmering patches of green and blue scales cover half of her face and her right arm—and probably more of her body that I can't see. She bears it like it's a shameful thing, but I think it's beautiful and I've always had a hunch the director agrees with me. When I'm in dragon form, I can always sense her emotions, but they're weaker than those from a fully-formed dragon. It's like trying to identify a shape through shower-door glass.

"How are you doing, Kitty?" Marcy's the kind of person who actually means it when she asks a question like this, so I feel compelled to give her an honest answer.

"Well, it's not my best day ever, but at least I'm doing better than this guy." I slap Wallace on the back.

Marcy makes a sympathetic tutting sound and shakes her

head, examining Wallace with kind eyes. "Anything I can do?"

He shakes his head without looking at her. After a minute, the silence starts to get super awkward.

Marcy pushes a crystal bowl sitting on her desk toward us. "Peanut butter cup?"

Wallace keeps his gaze on his feet, but I take a step forward. My fingers are an inch from chocolaty peanut-buttery goodness when a buzzing sound makes me jump back.

"He's ready for you now." Marcy stands and motions to the director's door. "Don't worry, I'm sure everything will be fine."

"Thanks, Marcy," I mutter before pushing Wallace through the door.

We find ourselves standing in front of the only human I truly fear: DIC Director John Bean, the only human allowed inside DIC complex. He's sitting in the tall, dark leather chair, but he's as intimidating as if he stands over me, glowering down. Unlike the rest of DIC, his office is rich with dark wood walls dramatically illuminated by up-lights rather than harsh fluorescents.

Most of this man's life is classified. He has enough scars to keep me guessing about his past, but they also make me too scared to ask about it. He stands tall and wide in a suit that *had* to be custom-made for him. Director Bean is the picture of discipline—from the top of his daily buzz cut to the toes of his spit-shined shoes. And he scares the freaking crap out of me.

Raising his head from reports on his desk, he motions for us to come inside with two flicks of a finger. He does not invite us to sit down. Wallace makes toward one of the black leather guest chairs but I catch his eye and give him a slight shake of my head in warning. Nobody sits in Director Bean's presence. I don't know any other mere human who can command so many dragons' respect and loyalty like him.

In the back corner of the office is a terrarium the size of a phone booth, the home to a half-dozen specimens of *draco volans*. *Draco volans* is also called the flying dragon, so named for a passing resemblance to some of my species. They have flaps of skin attached to rib extensions that allow them to glide like flying squirrels. These pets are the only evidence I've ever seen indicating Director Bean might have a sense of humor. It seems he has a cruel one, at least.

"Commander Lung tells me you both understand the gravity of our situation due to the events of last night, and that there's no need for me to discuss this," he says.

I only nod, wondering why I'm here if there is no reason to discuss the situation.

"However," he continues, "I told her that was impossible. Because if you understood how serious this was, it never would have happened." His voice only raises about half a decibel at the end of his statement, but the words thunder in my ears, bouncing around inside my head.

"Wallace." Director Bean levels the full force of his steel-gray eyes on the unfortunate English dragon. "Not only will you return to training status indefinitely, but you will also serve on cafeteria duty until further notice." Dragons don't trust humans enough to work inside the compound, so those of us who are injured or being disciplined do the housekeeping-type jobs.

I see Wallace's throat work up and down until he finally manages to croak out, "Yes, sir."

When the director meets my eyes, you can't convince me

he is human for anything. And they like to call *us* monsters. "And, Kitty," he says slowly. "You will not be permitted on any mission except when under the direct supervision of your commander."

He says "commander," but in a way that makes the underlying contempt obvious. What he means is: I won't be allowed off the leash without the direct supervision of my *mommy*.

"You will continue to serve as Midday Sun's"—Jacob's Secret Service code name—"bodyguard at the Academy until we can find a suitable replacement, but will return directly to D.I.C. immediately after the last bell. Are we clear?"

I clasp my hands together behind me in an attempt to dampen their shaking. "Yes, sir. Of course, sir."

He stands to his full height, making me feel even smaller than his words already have.

"Despite Simon's best efforts, we haven't yet been able to determine what the Lebanese government will do with the footage, but when they make their move, you should expect a full disciplinary hearing."

I swallow hard and stand as still as possible in front of the director, like prey freezing at the site of a predator, fearing that the tiniest movement might attract more of his attention than I care to possess.

"That is all. Do not be late for school. There's no reason to draw more attention than you already have."

I nod in obedience and take a last glance at the *draco volans*. One of the creatures leaps from one branch to another, but his wings don't catch any air. The glass cage isn't big enough for him to fly.

• • •

There are two exits from DIC. The one I never use starts with a huge underground parking lot that leads to a four-lane tunnel that dumps out onto an otherwise unused side road. Every now and then, a tourist will get lost and trip the proximity alarm, and we all have a bit of fun practicing a breach scenario. I don't have a car, so the only time I use this entrance is if I need to fly in hot and fast after a mission. After I turned sixteen, my mom talked about buying me a car, but I refused. Cars tether you to things like roads and parking lots. Not a fan.

The other entrance is a staircase up from the gym that leads to a manhole in a dense copse of trees a few stories above DIC. I'm sure, at some point, this was meant as a secret backup exit, but I use it every day. Sani, my partner and best friend, usually meets me here in the mornings and we race the ten miles to the Academy, splitting up for the last half mile so nobody sees us arrive together. The morning run helps us counteract the sluggishness that comes with sitting for eight hours in wooden chairs. But this morning I'm late, and he knows better than to wait and risk both of us being late. The mission must go on, after all.

I arrive at the designated meeting spot in front of the Academy half a second before Jacob's black Town Car with blacker windows pulls up. I whirl around, taking a quick less-than-covert survey of the area. Normally, I get here at least ten minutes early and do a better job of assessing the surroundings before he arrives.

Something dark flashes in the corner of my eye and I

know, without double-checking, that Sani's retreating into the building now that he sees he won't have to do my job today.

A suit-clad Secret Service agent steps out of the front passenger door, but Jacob climbs out of the backseat before the agent can reach his door—a blatant breach of protocol. I stifle a smile, knowing how much pleasure Jacob takes in even the smallest of rebellions. He shoots a grin at the agent who frowns pointedly at him. Not for the first time, I wonder if the Secret Service teaches their agents a class in how to frown with purpose. They do it really well when you call them "SS agents." They don't like that moniker—I worked that out myself.

"Hey Kitty!" he says to me, instantly forgetting about the two agents behind him. "You look like crap."

Pressing my lips together, I roll my eyes. "You sure know how to charm a girl."

He shrugs. "I don't get any complaints."

Though I'd never tell him so, I believe it. Even if you ignore the allure of a powerful father and his celebrity status, Jacob has the classically good-looking all-American-boy thing going on. He has sandy blond hair, honest blue eyes, and a smile that can make people throw themselves on railroad tracks for him. The perfect second-generation politician. It's not like I *like* him or anything. I know him too well. But every other girl in school makes gaga eyes at him when we walk down the hall.

"Hey, you wouldn't have anything to do with why my dad was up all night, having meetings with people I'm not even allowed to see, would you?"

"No idea what you're talking about," I say in an intentionally flat tone. I always obey my standing orders and deny any implication I'm anything more than the daughter of a wealthy Chinese diplomat, but do it in a way that lets Jacob know he's on the right track. It's a game we've been playing for three years, ever since I was put in his class to watch over him. The president told Jacob my family was important to relations with China and all but commanded him to befriend me. I, of course, have a different set of orders. And Jacob's way too smart to not realize something's up.

"Riiiight." He glances around us and lowers his voice to a whisper. "Seriously, Kitty, you have to tell me. It was a madhouse last night. What'd you do this time?"

"What makes you think it was me?"

He purses his perfect, full bow-shaped lips in that who-are-you-fooling kind of face. I look away and pick up the pace toward history class.

I'm not entirely sure how much information he's gleaned over the years, but he knows I have been put in place to protect him, and I'm stronger and faster than any girl my age (or any man ten years older, for that matter) has the right to be. Despite all our diligence, I've had to subvert a few kidnapping attempts last-minute. It seems he has a different theory every week as to where my talents come from. I believe genetically-engineered superhuman designed by the CIA is the reigning hypothesis lately. Please. Like the CIA knows anything about being extraordinary.

I haven't been to any others, since I grew up alternating between DIC headquarters and the most desolate places on earth, but I know this isn't an average high school. Sure, we have the standards like classrooms, teachers, and lockers. But our classrooms are redecorated by professional "educational environment specialists" every year, and every teacher has at least one PhD after their name. The kids walking down the halls have the self-important swagger inherited from their parents: diplomats, senators, CEOs, world-class thieves. I'm pretty confident of the last one, anyway.

"Hey, Sani!" Jacob calls to a tall, stunning boy walking toward us through the locker-lined hallway. Okay, well maybe it's just me he stuns.

I jerk up my head, mentally chiding myself for paying so little attention to our surroundings. But it isn't like Sani couldn't walk around unnoticed if he wanted to, despite his height. Bulisani Mathe is an African dragon, six feet two inches of stealth and grace with skin as dark as midnight. Jeans hang low on his hips, topped with a black uniform T-shirt. A gray hoodie hangs open across his chest, unfortunately hiding the lean muscles of his arms I have the pleasure of gawking at every time we spar.

Sani's my backup at the Academy, also getting a top-notch education in exchange for pledging life and allegiance to protect the president's son. Fortunately, I've never needed him, so Jacob still has no idea Sani's anything more than the equivalent of a Ugandan prince.

His eyes meet mine. I suck in a quick breath before regaining control of my suddenly hammering hearts. He smiles at me and for a second—just a second—I forget about last night, about my mom and the director, about everything but that tickling in my stomach. Gods, Kitty, you're a trained lethal operative; stop acting like a lovesick fool. I've had years of practice hiding my feelings for Sani underneath a thick blanket of other emotions.

I give Sani a (too) quick hug, and he shoots Jacob a friendly smile. Even in human form, dragon skin is almost hot enough to burn human skin so we always avoid direct contact with Jacob and the other students. Sani pretends he's germophobic, but I just pretend I don't like people too much. It's an easy facade for me. Sani lets Jacob walk ahead of him into history class and turns his face briefly to me, giving me a look that can't mean anything other than "we need to talk." I give him a quick nod and we take our seats in the back row just as the late bell rings.

Much to Jacob's chagrin, I always insist on sitting in the back of the classroom if I have the choice. He may like everyone staring at him, but I can't override my training and give up a tactical advantage like being able to see the entire room.

Mrs. Hall is ten minutes into a lecture on the Trail of Tears and I'm twenty pages into the latest celebrity gossip rag on my phone — my one guilty pleasure, so sue me — when a folded square of notebook paper lands on my desk. I know it came from Sani. No one else can get that close to me without my sensing it. I glance at Jacob to make sure he won't see and nearly laugh when I see him playing a game on his cell phone underneath his desk. Yeah, real Leader-of-the-Free-World material there. I unfold the note and lay it flat on my open history book.

What's going on? Heard a rumor this morning. Didn't hear much, just "Kitty", "Wallace" and "disaster." I wince. That's the gist of it, all right.

I glance toward Sani sitting on my right. Okay, if I'm honest, it's more than a glance — it always is when I look at him — but that's not the point. If I didn't know better, I'd think he's completely engrossed in Mrs. Hall's lecture — not waiting for my response with marked impatience. I scribble on the bottom of the note, casting my eyes up at the teacher occasionally so it looks like I'm just taking notes. I take my time deciding what to tell Sani, knowing this could be picked up by the teacher if we're caught. Sure, I should make him wait until after class, but I can never help wanting to give him what he asks for as soon as possible.

I write something, erase it. Try again, erase that. Sani coughs quietly and I scowl at him. I finally settle on:

Wallace changed. On camera. End of life as we know it?

That's vague enough.

I sit back and leave the note laying on my desk, knowing how much less noticeable it will be if Sani reaches over for it than if I try a clumsy pass-off.

I watch Mrs. Hall for a minute and when I glance back down at my desk, the note is gone. Sani shifts almost imperceptibly. I hear his two hearts beat harder, faster. Sure that he stares at me now, I shrug.

"Later," I murmur. No reason to draw attention to ourselves more than necessary.

Jacob's head snaps up and stares at the two of us with the light of a question in his eyes. He never cares for not being the center of attention in our little group, but I know he's starting to notice secrets between Sani and me. We're getting comfortable; we need to be more careful. Though I guess it won't matter so much if Bean pulls me off this assignment. I smile dismissively at him and pretend to turn my full attention to Mrs. Hall.

• • •

Government class in a D.C. school full of politicians' kids is a fresh new version of hell every day. Especially when you're already simply known as "that weird, quiet Asian girl." Even worse, this is the only class I have without Jacob or Sani. Our Secret Service contact thought it would blow our cover if we were placed in every single class with Jacob, so we each have one class without him. I'm not convinced one class is enough to dispel suspicion, but he's the expert, right? I mean, I've only been trained for this sort of thing since birth.

The bell finally rings and I send up a prayer of thanks that I made it through at least one class discussion without saying anything too moronic. Maybe I shouldn't take this stance, considering my job, but I hate politics. I can't stand that it's not something you can truly learn. There is no right or wrong answer. But then again, I can't tell if I hate politics because I hate this class, or vice versa. Back in the days of Imperial China, the rulers were all dragons. They were open about it, too, with their "dragon thrones" and "dragon beds" and all that, but modern scholars believe it was all a farce to instill fear and loyalty in the people. Personally, I'm not interested in ruling anybody.

I shove my untouched notebook back into my backpack and head to lunch.

Jacob is still in line for lunch when Sani joins me at our usual table in the dining room. Not a cafeteria, let's make that clear. The Academy has a schmancy dining room com-plete with mahogany—or whatever—tables, padded arm chairs, and antique vases for decoration. Thank the Gods they stopped short of making it full-service.

"Who caught it on camera?" he asks, getting straight to business. Unlike me, a direct descendant of the founders of DIC, Sani is a first-generation DIC operative. He still has one of those thick accents you can't quite place, overlaying a voice as smooth and subtle as his movements. He fled Uganda when his parents were murdered five years ago and found out about DIC through a distant cousin. DIC offered him housing, training, education—things he never had in Africa, even despite giving everything for his government. Like most of our operatives, he wants to give back to the country that gave him a safe place to call home and started training when he was twelve. In addition to CIA-mandated missions, DIC is also the only organization in the world that helps weredragons establish a normal (as possible) life. As a result, most dragons live in the United States, even though there aren't any native to here as far as I can tell. Dragon history is spotty at best, owing to our solitary natures. Before DIC formed, no more than two adult dragons lived in the same place at one time. That's probably how we've gone so long without being discovered, I imagine.

I tell Sani as much as I can about last night for the next four minutes while tracking Jacob's slow process through the lunch line, hindered by all the people who stop to talk to him. Even as I'm telling the story, I notice how Jacob talks to everyone—including the scholarship kids—with the same easy smile and genuine friendliness. No one talks to the scholarship kids. He's a friend to these people; he's a friend to me. This sudden heartbreaking realization hits me, and I stumble in the story I'm telling. It may be my duty to protect him, but I *want* to do it, too. It's the only mission I've ever given my heart to and, once Director Bean is done with me, DIC is going to take it away from me.

"Kitty?" Sani says. "You there?" He's waving a hand twice the size of my own in front of my face.

I've entirely stopped talking, and my hands are clenched so tightly on the edges of my lunch tray the plastic is starting to warp. The dragon inside me rages against my emotional control. It wants to be let out. Heck, I want to let it out, but I know that wouldn't exactly fix anything. It's only through force of will that I loosen my grip and give Sani a small smile.

When I tell Sani about the meeting with Director Bean this morning he says, "There was nothing you could have done."

He places a warm, reassuring hand over mine, and both of my hearts skip a beat or two when I meet his totally, weirdly beautiful eyes. Like those of all African dragons, they're a strange yellow-green color with elongated pupils—almost like a cat's but not enough so that you'd notice when passing him on the street. That's probably because African dragons look more like a black cat-salamander hybrid than any dragon you've ever imagined; they have a lightly furred catlike head on top of a long, slender four-legged body.

"Done about what?" Jacob drops his tray noisily across the table from me. I jump and yank my hand away from Sani's.

"I got a C on that English paper Mr. Sadler handed back today," I say. This is total bull. Blessed with a dragon's intelligence, I have to intentionally make mistakes to get anything less than an A on any assignment.

Jacob laughs and takes a swig of his apple juice. "The way your faces looked, you'd think the world was ending."

I fake a laugh that emptily echoes his. "Yeah, I guess when you put it into perspective…"

Sani shoots me a look before changing the subject. "Have either of you met the new girl?" He nods toward a table on the other side of the dining room where a blond girl sits by herself, pushing food around her plate.

"I've seen her in the halls," I say. "She just started today?"

Sani nods once. "Must be why she's eating lunch alone."

Don't get jealous that he noticed her, Kitty. Of course he noticed; he always notices things like that. That's part of what makes him such a good partner, remember? You want him to notice things.

The little pep talk does nothing to dampen the raging jealousy stabbing at my stomach.

Jacob stands up. "That's a shame," he says, grinning. "We should be a little more welcoming."

"Yeah," I say knowingly. "She is pretty cute, isn't she?"

"I don't know what you're talking about." Jacob winks at me. "I'm just trying to be friendly."

Sani shakes his head. "He'll make a great politician someday."

"America's had much worse," I say.

As a general rule, no one ever joins our little group for very long. It isn't a policy—it really isn't even on purpose—but it turns out teenagers aren't a big fan of background checks on everyone they know just so they can hang out with somebody. And the body searches? Not the most popular. Not even the Senators' kids are exempt from the precautions—and most of them can't stand to be subjected to the same standards as "normal" people.

In about ten seconds Jacob has the blond girl following him across the cafeteria, her tray balanced on his right hand. He tries to guide her by placing his left hand on her back, but she pulls away with a shy smirk. His smile doesn't even waver at the slight, and he beams at us when they reach our table.

"Kitty, Sani," Jacob nods at each of us when he says our names. "This is Gesina."

I instantly realize I had been wrong in my previous assessment; she isn't just cute, she's gorgeous. I mean the high-end-magazine-cologne-ad kind of gorgeous. Flawless lightly tanned skin, eyebrows plucked to perfection, shimmering hair the color of sunlit wheat, blue eyes that seem to glow from within. She is the most beautiful human I have ever seen.

I fight back the wry look I have for Jacob and smile. "Hey."

"Very nice to meet you," Sani says, then throws me a glance. "Gesina…?"

I know what he's getting at; the paperwork the Secret Service requires when a new person starts spending time with Jacob is insane. We need at least a last name to start the process, and I really don't want to break into the musty old student record filing cabinet again.

"Sorry?" she says with a delicate tilt of her blond eyebrows. Her heavy accent dominates even that one word, distorting the two syllables. Gesina is decidedly German, and I suddenly understand why Jacob is grinning so widely; as much as the Secret Service hates when Jacob takes in strays, it's even worse if they aren't American.

"What's your last name?" I clarify.

She glances around as if caught in a trap. Subtlety has never been one of my strong suits.

Sani rushes to cover for me. "Your homeroom is decided by your last name," he explains. "We were just wondering if you're in one of ours." Somehow, I'm still occasionally caught off guard by how smoothly Sani lies. We all have the same homeroom—it'd been arranged by the Secret Service—and both of us knew she wasn't in it. For as noble and thoughtful as he is, he can spin untruths with the best of them.

"Ah, of course," she says, her body language returning to normal. She smirks a tiny bit. "Fuchs."

"Oh, not in my homeroom. Too bad. Please, sit down," Sani says.

Jacob plops her tray on the table and she sits between me and the First Son. Sani sends me a look and a jerk of his head obviously meant to say it's my turn to call this one in. It amazes me how much Sani and I can communicate using only looks and glances after the past three years on Jacob's detail. I sit through a few more minutes of the obligatory getting-to-know-you questions (Where are you from? What grade are you in? Do you play any sports?) before excusing myself.

"Little girl's room," I say with an apologetic shrug as I gather up my lunch tray and stand. "See you next period."

Jacob gives me a single wave without removing his gaze from Gesina's face. Sani nods and Gesina says, "*Tschüss.*"

I grimace a little at her use of German. If Gesina lasts very long, the Secret Service will probably make me learn how to speak it. Though if this morning's chat with the director is any indication, Gesina will last longer than I will. Soon, she'll become someone else's problem. A possessive ache pulses in my stomach.

Chapter Three

Five minutes left in the last class of the school day and I can't seem to keep myself still. The tension playing through my mind started as a gentle whisper but spent the day crescendoing to a disastrous clamor. I should have heard something by now, surely. After calling in for Gesina's file and to begin her background check, I called my mother for any news about the Lebanese embassy. Her phone went straight to voicemail. When I called Marcy's desk, the phone rang until I gave up after a few minutes. This was unprecedented.

I cross my legs underneath my desk, steal a glimpse of my DIC phone in my pocket, uncross my legs, lean back in my chair, lean forward. And still, a minute hasn't even passed. I try to focus on Mr. Sandhill's explanation of our next chemistry lab assignment, hoping it will make the time go faster. Big surprise: it doesn't. I conquered college-level chemistry when I was eight, after all. I can't even focus enough to finish up the article about Brangelina's latest humanitarian mission. That's how I know it's serious. Finally, mercifully, the bell rings.

I spring from my seat and take my first step toward the door in the same movement, but then I hear Jacob calling out to me.

"Kitty! Wait up!"

I groan under my breath, but wait out in the hallway for him. He comes out of the classroom wearing his this-smile-gets-me-anything-I-want smile.

"Oh, no. What do you want?" I ask.

"Why do you think I want something? Can't a guy just smile at his best friend?"

Sani had stopped to ask Mr. Sandhill a question, and he catches up with us now. "Best friend?" he asks Jacob, then turns to me. "What does he want?"

Jacob's incredulous face makes me laugh despite my eagerness to get back to DIC and check on the Lebanese situation. I cross my arms dramatically over my chest and raise one eyebrow. "That's what I was just trying to figure out."

"Okay, okay. You got me," Jacob says, holding up his hands in surrender. He tilts his head down and looks at me through his lashes, letting his voice turn husky. I've seen this work on just about every girl in school. "I was hoping you'd hang out with me tonight. Maybe we could grab dinner or watch a movie at the House or something. Sani can come too."

"Thanks so much for the warm invitation," Sani mutters good-naturedly.

Despite the flirtatious way he's approaching it, I know he's not asking me on a date. This is how he usually gets what he wants from girls—he forgets I'm not like most girls.

There's something more. I move closer to Jacob and sniff several times, circling him.

"What are you doing?" Jacob asks.

"I smell something fishy," I say, barely containing my laughter.

"Oh, forget it." Jacob waves a hand dismissively at us and spins on his heel toward the student pickup area.

"Wait," I call out, laughing. I take a few quick strides to catch up with him and keep pace on his right side. Sani joins us on his left side. "Seriously, what was that about?"

Jacob shifts his eyes to the right and then to the left to look at us, trying to decide if whatever he's holding back is worth telling us. He sighs. "I want to hang out with Gesina, and I was thinking it would be less awkward for her if there were other non-suits there."

"Oh," I say in a teasing tone, stretching the word out for several seconds. "I get it."

"Just forget about it," Jacob says again.

"Really, Jake. I'd love to go on a double date," I say. Sani's eyes widen momentarily, and there's no way I miss it. "But my mom's expecting me home right after school for some important family stuff."

Jacob looks with pleading eyes at Sani, who presses his full lips into a regretful frown. "Sorry, man. Doctor's appointment."

Jacob's shoulders slump ever so slightly but he's already too media-trained to let the entirety of his disappointment show.

"Maybe we can do it tomorrow?" Sani suggests. Then, after a slight shake of my head, "Or later this week."

Jacob looks down at the ground. "I already asked her.

And she said yes."

"You did? She did?" asks Sani.

We trade a worried glance behind his head. One of us has an eye on Jacob every second of the school day, and we hadn't seen him talk to Gesina since lunch.

"When?" I ask.

He pulls his cell phone from his pocket and wiggles it in front of Sani's face. "She slipped me her number at lunch and I texted her during chemistry. She's going to ride home with me, already got permission from her mom."

I try to dial down my anger before talking. Part of the anger is self-directed. I was too absorbed in my own worries to notice what he'd been doing in chemistry. "You're not supposed to release your phone number to anyone without prior security clearance."

"Release my number? Prior security clearance?" Jacob mocks. "Damn, Kitty. You sound like one of the suits."

"I—" I begin, but stop myself before revealing something I shouldn't. I swallow and begin again. "I'm just concerned about you. You know, as your *best friend*."

Jacob scoffed. "It'll be fine. She's just one girl and I'll be with suits the whole time."

Three-wide, we burst through double doors out into the sunniest day of the year so far. March in D.C. isn't exactly known for its sunshine, so all three of us take a moment to tilt our heads toward the warm rays bathing us in light so bright our eyes slam shut.

"Jacob!" Gesina calls from halfway down the stairs.

Jacob speeds up to meet her; Sani and I trail a little behind, giving each other wary looks behind his back. Gesina beams at Jacob, then looks at me. "Are you going to hang out with us at Jacob's house?"

I stare at her for a second before answering. She doesn't seem at all nervous that she's about to go "hang out" with the president's son—and his full complement of bodyguards. I know she's fresh-off-the-boat—or plane, whatever—German, but surely she knows who he is, right? Maybe it's possible she doesn't realize Jacob's house is actually The White House? Regardless of their nationality, teenage humans confuse the pants off me.

"No," I say. "Prior engagements." I shrug and try to make it look apologetic.

"Too bad," she says with regret, but her body betrays a different sentiment. Her shoulders lift slightly and she raises her chin a fraction of an inch. I allow a smirk to tickle my lips; the girl wants Jacob all to herself. I usually despair a little for the girls Jacob chooses to wear around his pinkie finger for a while, but I think: this one? She may be able to hold her own. She might even give him a small taste of his own medicine.

An awkward silence wraps its heavy arms around our little group as Sani and I escort Jacob to his waiting car with no less than three Secret Service agents waiting to transport him. Jacob waves good-bye to us as he climbs in the car. The agent standing at the door tries to close it then, but Jacob stops him with grin.

"I have a guest riding with me today," he says, gesturing toward Gesina.

"Sir," the agent sighs like he's done it a thousand times that day. "That is entirely against protocol."

Jacob's pout is so heartrending that I might believe it was genuine if I knew him a tiny bit less. "Now, Dominic. We wouldn't want to be rude to the German ambassador's only daughter, would we?"

I see about seven stages of conflict cross over Dominic's face in the space of three heartbeats. Gesina steps forward and looks the agent straight in the eye.

"If it's too much trouble," she says, "we can try another day."

A tingle sweeps over my skin, like the hum of static on a speaker after the music stops.

Jacob opens his mouth to object to Gesina's suggestion when Dominic speaks. "No, that's okay. You're welcome to ride with us."

"What?" I ask quietly, but nobody pays me any attention.

"We're all set then," Jacob says, waving for Gesina to join him in the car.

The German girl is standing a few feet to my right side. "Great," she says.

Then, she surprises me by turning her body to face me. "Maybe next time," she says and I can tell there is genuine regret behind those words. Her perfectly manicured hand reaches out to gently touch my arm. I instinctively jerk away, but she's still somehow able to rest her hand on my wrist for about half a second.

I suddenly feel like I'm lost in a forest I've walked through many times. I stare at a point in front of me that I'm not entirely sure exists. But it must, because I can't seem to tear my gaze away.

"Kitty!" Sani is calling my name, but he sounds like he's above the waves of this ocean that's drowning me in nothing. Now I can almost see him, standing in front me, shaking my shoulders as if to wake me. The world comes back into focus and the first thing I see is Jacob's car about to turn onto the main road at the end of the half-mile driveway from the Academy.

Sani's touch on my shoulders fully snaps me back to reality. His hands are hot enough to burn human skin, like a dragon's hands should be. Like Gesina's hand had been.

Chapter Four

I fumble in my pocket for my Secret Service phone and dial the number for my contact while Sani stares at me, still waiting for an explanation of my spacing out a few seconds ago. My contact answers.

"This is Draco Three. Probable threat."

"What—" Sani begins. I cut him off with a glare and, within half of a heartbeat, a confused realization dawns on his face.

"In Midday Sun's car. Now." I don't say much, but it's enough for my contact, whose name I don't actually know.

He pauses for maybe three seconds. It feels like an eternity. "Communication with the agents in the car is down. Can you pursue on foot?"

I start running at the word "down" and I'm already half-way down the driveway with Sani at my side when I say, "Pursuing."

"Secure Midday Sun," my contact orders. "At all costs."

"Understood." I don't bother hanging up before dropping both the phone and my backpack on the grass. Sani has already shed his pack.

The car is gaining speed on the main road, but traffic is keeping it from escaping completely. I can run about twenty miles an hour for several miles. Sani is faster. He's holding back to stay with me.

"Go!" I yell.

I know he wants to argue, but I'm not his friend right now. I'm his superior. To his credit, he doesn't hesitate longer than the time it takes for a single step. His stride lengthens. It's a matter of seconds before he's halfway between me and the car.

The front half of the black Town Car explodes in a fireball. My lungs are working overtime, and I gulp in the acrid scent of burning rubber and gasoline. Tires all around us squeal as brakes are slammed. Somewhere to my left, a roaring crunch echoes the explosion, as two more cars collide in a less explosive way.

Dominic pops out of the sunroof, somehow looking confused and focused at the same time. He has his side arm in his right hand, and I dare to hope the Secret Service has control of the situation. But, somewhere inside me, I know better.

Dominic raises his gun and takes aim at Sani, who's fifty feet from the car. He fires four shots.

I let loose a primal roar as a bullet rips through Sani's left bicep. His shoulder jerks back at the impact, but his steps don't even falter.

Why the hell is Dominic shooting at us? He knows who we are. Unless he's in on the whole thing. My dragon self bellows to be let loose like it never has before. The beginning of the change scratches at my fingertips. Only my need to help Sani lets me suppress the urge to change. Letting the dragon take control of the change wouldn't benefit any of us.

A flicker of movement on the left side of the car seizes my attention. Gesina is dragging a dazed Jacob out of the car. She's having less trouble with his weight than I would have expected from such a waif of a girl. I alter course to intercept her.

Dominic—the bastard looking steady and calm—pops off another round. I don't see where the bullet strikes.

But I do see, out of the corner of my eye, Sani's body crashing to the asphalt a few feet from the back bumper.

It takes every freaking shred of control I have not to run to him. My soul fights me, tugging toward him like a physical force inside me. I can smell his blood. It's coppery with hints of iron and earth, and there's too much of it. But I still have a job to do.

Gesina shoves Jacob to the side seconds before I tackle her at full speed. We tumble violently, the asphalt snatching at our skin and clothes. She grasps for my arm three times before she catches it and latches on. I barely have time to register her touch before I'm lost in that forest again.

I know I want to stand up and do...something. But I don't think my body would respond even if I knew what it was. A vibration trembles on the edge of my thoughts, beating at a steady pace.

The confusion abandons me as suddenly as it came. I'm lying on my back, my arms twisted underneath me, staring at a helicopter hovering only a couple of dozen feet up. I don't see Jacob, but Gesina is pulling herself into the copter from a hanging rope ladder. There's something strange about her shape and, when she heaves her torso into the helicopter, I see what looks like a long white fluffy tail hanging from her butt.

WTF? I blink a few times to clear my sight. I catch one last glimpse of the tail as Gesina hauls her legs into the helicopter. Once she's inside, it tilts to turn north. I see Jacob's familiar profile strapped into one of the seats, his head hanging limp and bobbing with the movement of the copter.

Despite my confusion, my training kicks in and I find myself examining the helicopter for identifying marks. Nothing. I mean, absolutely nothing, all black with no markings on the machine or the people inside it. It's definitely not legal to fly that thing inside the city limits.

The helicopter is out of sight before I'm able to move more than my head. My dragon strains against my consciousness, clamoring to pursue Gesina. I jump to my feet and scan the crowd that has gathered around us and the burning car. Three burly Good Samaritan types are hauling the slightly blackened Secret Service agents out of the car. At least half of the people have their cell phones out, taking videos and pictures to post to Facebook and Twitter. Crap. There's no way I can change here. Even if I turned on the invisibility mode as soon as I changed, there would be a fraction of a second my dragon form would be exposed, and someone would catch the image, I'm sure. Two Number One rule violations in twenty-four hours probably wouldn't be good for my health.

Sani groans and rolls to his back. I run to him. When I see a giant red-soaked spot on his chest, I trip over my own damned feet and stumble to a stop on the ground next to him.

"Sani?" I peel his sticky shirt back to expose a bloody hole marring his otherwise perfect chest. I notice the first shot, a through and through on his bicep, has already healed.

"I'm all right," he says, but I can't imagine how that's even close to the truth.

I wipe the warm blood away as best as I can with my hands to get a better look at the wound. Dragons heal fast, and he's already stopped bleeding, but it's awfully close to…

"Did it hit your—" I choke on a sob and cough to cover it up.

"Yeah," he says. "It hit my left heart. I think it's just a nick, though. Still beating."

While in human form, a second heart is redundant. We can live if one of them is damaged, but it takes both hearts to maintain dragon form and we can't change if one is even a little injured.

A few annoying, but well-intentioned, members of the crowd move closer to us, and sirens sound a mile or two away. Movement in the wound catches my eye and I lean over Sani, as close as I can, to shield him from the crowd around us. I tangle my legs in his and wrap my arms around his neck, as if we're lovers. As if.

I dream of being this close to Sani every day, but I never wanted it to be like this. His eyes dart to my lips then back to my eyes before he says anything. "What are you—" His question is cut short by a grunt of pain low in his throat. "Oh." He wraps his right arm around my waist and his arm tightens in pain. His fingers dig into my skin, but I don't mind.

The bullet wiggles its way out of the wound and I slide my hand along his torso to his chest to catch it before anyone around us can see. It's kinda slimy and disgusting, but I don't let it show on my face. Dragons' bodies always reject any foreign material this way; we can't even pierce our ears, and tattoos are way out of the question. I've seen something like this happen a few hundred times before, but I know it's not something human bodies do, and we don't need any more questions.

I stare into Sani's eyes, enjoying the view while I'm here. His wound doesn't worry me as much anymore; he's breathing steadily, and he has no symptoms of shock.

"Kitty," Sani says. "We have to go."

I look around at all the people—*no, use the proper term; they're witnesses now*—surrounding the car and the two of us. "We can't. How are we going to explain this?"

"We have to," he whispers. "And now. We need to call the Secret Service and DIC so they can get on this right away. They may even be able to intercept the helicopter if we're fast enough."

He's right and I know it, even if I don't like it. "Can you run?" I ask, trying to assess his health with a glance at his wound. It's starting to close up.

"Yeah. I'm in top shape," he says, smirking. "I can outrun you."

"Don't make me make you eat your words, Mathe," I say. "Pull your hood up. Straight for our packs, then inside the school to the photo lab. Don't stop for anything. Ready?"

He nods.

"One. Two. Three."

• • •

Sani's true to his word and beats me to the photo lab by a couple seconds. Though I know he's not in top shape; if that were true, he would have been here before I got in the building. There had been a few confused shouts when we started running, but nobody followed us in time to find us in the windowless room of the photo lab. We dart inside and lock the solid steel door. I pull out my Secret Service phone and my thumb hovers over the dial button. Even in my often-imagined worst-case scenarios, this is a call I never thought I'd have to make. My hand shakes and the phone's screen goes out of focus.

Sani knows why I hesitate. "I can do it," he offers.

It's truly tempting, but I know it would be wrong. This is my responsibility.

My contact picks up before the end of the first ring. "Draco Three?" For the first time in three years, he doesn't sound bored.

"We lost him." I try to keep all emotion out of my voice, and I have no idea if I succeed.

"Dammit!" my contact shouts, and I hear a loud crash in the background. I flinch at the sound. Sani wraps a strong arm around my shoulders and pulls me to his side.

"Draco Four was shot. I was…" What was I? Bewitched? Entranced? I thought Gesina was a dragon, but I've never seen a dragon with a long white fluffy tail. And only Chinese dragons have special abilities. What should I tell him? I'll be in enough debriefings after this without them thinking I'm delusional. "I'll file a full report later."

I give my contact the immediately salient details and hang up, sliding the phone into my pocket. If that helicopter is still in the air, they'll find it. They have to.

"Now for the scary part." I force a laugh to conceal the lump in my throat. "I have to tell my mom I screwed up a second mission within twenty-four hours."

My voice wavers as I speak, betraying emotions I've spent years learning to suppress. This is why they warn against getting close to assignments. My mind keeps showing me Jacob's limp form soaring away from me as I stand there, helpless. I clench my fists to keep my hands from shaking.

Taking a deep, slow breath, I focus on what I can do. I dig around in my backpack for my DIC phone, a new-model Android. My Secret Service one is a crappy bare-bones flip phone—figures. I unlock the screen but, before I can dial, I see a text message waiting for me. I don't recognize the number. I tap the icon and it says:

Check CNN. Don't come home. Don't respond. Ditch this phone now.—Number One

The voice message icon sits at the top of the screen, but that's no surprise; I never check those. Anyone who has ever met me knows to text me instead. Even Director Bean has Marcy text me if he really needs me right away. She doesn't always get the shorthand right, but I appreciate that she tries.

I show the message to Sani. "Number One?" he asks.

"Wallace. It's what they were calling him because of last night's mission." I make for the door. Sani grabs my arm to stop me.

"Check CNN," he says, motioning to the text still on the screen. How does he always manage to stay so calm? I feel like a bull in a china closet next to his steady form.

"Why? It's probably news about Jacob. I don't want to

see that."

He raises his eyebrows just a little and glances to my Android. "The time stamp was for ten minutes ago, before they even got in the car."

I sigh and open up the browser, not wanting to see the consequences of my latest mistake splattered across the headlines. CNN's website is very mobile-friendly so the picture related to their top story displays in seconds. It's a still from the Lebanese security camera.

Of Wallace just after changing.

Simply seeing this knocks the breath out of my lungs. I've always heard people say that their blood ran cold, but could never really imagine how that would feel. I thought it was just a human thing. Now I know it's not. I shiver from the force of it.

The headline underneath reads, "U.S. admits to existence of dragon shapeshifters after video leak." And below that one, "President assures all dragons are now confined and under control." And finally, "Dragons aren't a hoax." Every one of these stories has been posted in the last hour. I don't tap on them to read them. I don't need to; I know what they say.

Sani reads silently over my shoulder. The scent of blood and sweat overpowers the always-present chemical stench in the lab. He's stunned for a minute, then finally manages one word. "Confined?"

We both sort of glare at the picture for a while, hoping to make it not true with the force of our stares. It doesn't work.

"If this is true, they're probably looking for us," Sani says. And he knows a thing or two about governments tracking him down. "Check your voicemail."

I have two messages from today. One from my mother—who may sound normal to everyone else but I can hear the distress in her voice—telling me I've been immediately recalled and I need to come home. She's given me thousands of orders over the years; I can tell she doesn't mean this one. The second message is from a male voice I don't recognize. He says he's with the CIA and I need to come home right away. For my own protection.

Right. There aren't many certainties in my world but I know this: when someone says they're doing something for your protection, it's complete and total BS.

"My guess is they're all being held by the CIA. How did Wallace get a message to you?" Sani asked.

I shrug. "Someone must have been stupid enough to leave him alone with a computer or cell phone. Most people don't realize that passwords don't protect you from someone like Wallace."

"Okay." I can see the resignation take over as Sani says this. "Ditch the phone, like he says. They can track it. I'll leave mine here, too."

"Yeah." GPS tracking is only accurate to one hundred feet. "Let them search every supply closet and crawl space in this school."

"Should you drop the Secret Service phone, too?"

It's a legit question. Should I? SS phones are bounced off a gazillion satellites and not easily traceable—but if anyone outside of DIC could do it, the CIA could. The number isn't written anywhere. Only three people know it: the president, Jacob, and my contact. And if anyone does find out the number? They can back-trace it to a man named Jethro Johnson in Beaver Creek, Montana. It's the only way I have of contacting any of them. But can I trust them not to turn me in?

"No," I say. "I'll keep it for now."

I grab the phone he's holding out, throw both of the DIC phones in the chemical supply closet, and latch the door.

"All right, let's get out of here." If I keep moving, maybe I won't completely freak out. I know myself well enough. If I think too much about the last sixteen hours, I won't be able to leave this room.

Sani looks ready to burst out of the door, but then turns to me with his eyebrows squished together over his wide nose. "Where are we going?"

"Gesina's house."

"Is that wise?" my careful, calm Sani says. "There's a good chance we're being hunted, and we're just going to stroll up to an ambassador's house?"

"What did the president say?" I throw up air quotes. "'*All* dragons are confined and under control.' We know he knows about us. He's lying. The CIA may be looking for us, but they don't want most people to know it, certainly not foreign officials. Besides, her name's the only lead we have at this point."

Sani's lips tighten in concentration. "You're probably right. But let's get a change of clothes from the athletic department before we head out. The pictures and videos from the abduction are probably all over the internet by now."

"Yeah." I motion to the dark red Rorschach on his shirt. "And you're a mess."

As we head out into the hallway, Sani asks, "What are the chances Gesina returned to her house after kidnapping the president's son?" It's a rhetorical question.

We're foot soldiers, not strategists. Both of us are used to waiting for orders and doing only what it takes to carry them out. But my entire command structure is out of commission, and I just can't sit here while that girl gets away with my friend.

"Gesina's address is the one solid piece of information I have right now. I have to do something. Unless you have a better idea?"

Sani's mouth sets into a hard line and he shakes his head. "Let's go."

Chapter Five

"Gesina isn't home," the ex-NFL-wannabe in a monkey suit tells Sani. The German ambassador's house is one of the older brick buildings in downtown D.C., converted to a swank loft-style condo. This guy apparently stands inside the door just to say "boo" to whoever knocks.

"Of course she's not," I mumble. "Because she's out kidnap—oomph." Sani's elbow to my stomach stops the words in my throat.

I hadn't dared to hope the girl would make it easy on us by coming home, but any information we can find out is better than the diddly-squat we currently have. I stare at the sweat dripping down the forehead of this very human security guard and wonder how a dragon ended up the daughter of a German ambassador. Was she adopted? Or is the ambassador an undocumented dragon, too? Dragons are naturally solitary and suspicious creatures, so nobody really knows how many are prowling about, masquerading as humans. "Do you have any idea when she'll be home? She left this assignment at school," Sani says as he pulls a random piece of paper out of his backpack. "It's due tomorrow; I'd hate for her to get a bad grade on it." His eyes are so earnest that I almost believe it, and I suddenly hate how this job has made a liar out of him. When I first met him, he couldn't have told a lie to save his life—and now he has to do just that over and over again. "Do you think I'm dumb enough to give out the ambassador's daughter's schedule to total strangers?" the goon asks.

Yes.

"No, of course not," I say, faking the most convincing innocent-little-girl smile I can muster. "We understand. We'll come back later."

"I can take the paper and give it to Miss Ammon when she gets home," monkey-suit offers. So kind of him.

Miss who?

"Give what to me, Joe?" I whirl around at the sound of Gesina's thick accent and it takes every scrap of self-control my mother forced into me not to tear her lungs out right there on the stoop.

"Oh, I'll give it to you, you little bitch." So much for self-control. I lunge at Gesina with my arms outstretched—only to restrain her, of course—but Sani and his damned reflexes stop me before I've taken a step. His arms encircle me like a steel band, unmovable.

"What are you doing?" I hiss between my teeth.

"Trust me?" Sani says gently, slightly loosening his grip, testing me.

A glance behind me shows the goon with his hand on his sidearm. I relax a little. I guess it wouldn't be the best thing to cause a scene with all these cameras and armed guards around. Sani drops his arms to his side and takes a small step toward the girl.

"I'm sorry," Gesina says softly. She crosses her arms to stop them from shaking and casts a glance at the bodyguard every half a second. What happened to all this girl's confidence? "Do I know you?"

"Gesina Ammon?" Sani says.

She pauses halfway through her nod, like she's not sure if she should admit it to the nice guy with the psychotic companion.

"Please excuse my friend here, she has a neurological condition and can't control herself." I snort, but he continues. "I'm Bulisani Mathe."

He stretches his hand out as if to shake hers, and she reluctantly offers her own in return. I watch a wave of shock travel from her mouth, through her eyes, to end in raised eyebrows. She is surprised at the temperature of his hand, and he pulls it back quickly so he doesn't hurt her.

"I'm sorry, there seems to be some mistake," he says dismissively, already backing away toward the street.

"What?" I say, mind spinning in confusion. "There's no mistake. That's her. Different last name, but same girl."

He grabs my arm and pulls me close so our heads are cheek-to-cheek, both of us looking at the girl. "Kitty, seriously. Calm down for a sec and look at her," he whispers.

I take a deep breath and do as Sani asks—mainly because I can hardly deny him anything he asks of me. Especially when he's touching me in no less than two places. Gah, focus, Kitty.

I look closely at Gesina. She looks the same. Doesn't

she?

As my temper fades, I start seeing little differences. She has a few pimples and blackheads on her face. Her eyes aren't as bright as I remember. Her lips are uneven with the top lip being too thin for the full bottom lip. She's still pretty, but nothing like the angel I met in the lunchroom. The confidence and self-assuredness is replaced by a marked shyness.

"Gesina?"

She jumps at her name. A trace of guilt flits through my consciousness over scaring this poor girl. I try to give her a friendly smile, but it's not something I have a lot of practice with.

"Do you have a sister?" I ask. "A twin, maybe?"

"My sister is four and she lives in Germany," she says. "I came here to go to university. What is this about?" Her voice raises an octave with worry.

"You're not who we're looking for. I apologize. Have a nice day." Sani takes my arm and half-drags me down the sidewalk.

I toss a look over my shoulder as she turns to go inside, checking one last time for any trace of a tail. "Well, that was a dead end."

"Maybe not."

"Umm, were you part of the same conversation I was?" I ask.

"When I shook her hand—"

He pauses, so I interrupt. "It was human temperature. I saw the shock on her face when you touched."

I don't want to admit the next part, because it means we really are at a dead end. But it has to be said, to make it real. "That's not the same girl who took Jacob."

He sighs and nods, running a hand over his face. When his hand reaches back to rub his neck, my eyes jealously track his movements.

"So who is she?" I say. "Why does kidnapper Gesina look like the movie-star version of innocent Gesina?"

"You got your Secret Service contact to pull her school file, right?" There's no accusation in his voice.

We cross the street to catch the bus to—well, I don't really know where we're going yet. "Yeah," I say.

"She was posing as Gesina *Fuchs*, the German ambassador's daughter."

Oo-oh. "But the ambassador's daughter is Gesina Ammon," I say.

Sani stares into space, thinking. "It's a strange mistake. Everything else was so professional. How could they get something so easy so wrong?"

"More importantly, how could the SS not catch that the second they pulled her file?"

"Two possible answers. Someone on the inside helped with Jacob's abduction." He raises his hand to rub his closely cropped hair again and I hope this isn't true, because it would destroy the last string of faith he's hanging from. It took him forever to trust a government again, after what happened to his parents. He still doesn't go hook, line, and sinker on every line Director Bean dangles in front of us as it is.

"Or someone who's able to fool the Secret Service is backing her up."

He stops walking, probably realizing we don't know where we're going. The silence between us hangs heavy with doubt and regret.

"How's your heart?" I finally ask.

A faraway look takes over his features as he looks inward, talking with his dragon-self. "It's healing, but I can't change yet. Soon."

I nod and Sani looks to me, ready to follow my lead. I don't want to tell him I have no idea where to go. He needs a safe place to heal, and I need to figure out our next move, but all my usual safe places are compromised, and I'm not sure who I can trust. The idea flashes through my mind like a lightning bolt. There may be one person left who can help me.

"You know, my father claims tea can cure anything." I allow myself a smile as a thread of hope returns to my thoughts. "And I know where to find the best."

Sani raises his eyebrow like he knows there's more to what I'm saying, but doesn't object. "Bus?" He motions to the bus stop half a block down the street.

My skin itches with the idea of being trapped in one of those metal cases again. My dragon rears her head in my chest, yearning to be set free. Poor Sani. Not being able to change, even temporarily, must be torture. Even when I'm stuck in human form for a long time, just knowing my dragon is waiting there under the surface brings me peace.

I look around the neighborhood until I spot an empty, obviously foreclosed house with an overgrown backyard, shielded even more by the long shadows cast by the setting sun.

"No." I nearly grin now. "Let's fly."

Chapter Six

We're flying half a mile above Chinatown, Sani on my back, invisible to the people below, when I spot the familiar tea shop. Warm light floods out onto the street through the smeared and dusty windows. My dragon body is curved into an *S* shape to help make Sani's ride more comfortable. I manipulate the magnetic fields around me and control our descent into the back alley, where I fly into the truck-sized delivery door and hit the button to close the garage door with a flick of my tail. Curled as I am, I fit easily inside the space. As soon as the last sliver of street and moon light is snuffed out by the door, Sani slides off my back and I snap back to human form.

The few humans who know about us always ask me how I manage to shift back with all the clothes and personal belongings I started with. I give the same answer every time: magic. But I'm dragon enough to admit my answer's a defense mechanism to cover the fact I have absolutely no freaking clue. Like I don't know how we break this "conservation of mass" principle the scientists are always going on about. We're *dragons*. Simon and some of his egghead friends have a theory that involves quantum mechanics. He thinks we don't change our bodies so much as store the one we're not using—and all the stuff it's holding—in a parallel plane of existence. He claims our bodies, running hot and with two hearts, are something like a quantum generator. It makes sense when he explains it, but it's not exactly something that's easy to prove.

"You seem like you know your way around this place. Where are we?" Sani asks. He looks around the storage room, but there's only the light shining between the door cracks, and even our excellent dragon sight can only make out long, dark shadows.

"Well, you've met the great Commander Lung." I move to the door that leads into the shop.

His eyes grow to the size of plums as he realizes what I mean. "I'm going to meet your father?" He immediately starts straightening out his shirt, which is totally ridiculous considering the permanent creases from being stuffed in the basketball team's storage bin. He runs his hands over his hair, as if he has enough to be out of place to start with. It's pretty adorable, if I'm being honest with myself.

He fidgets awkwardly. It's the first time I've ever seen him lose his signature cool, and I laugh. And immediately feel guilty when I remember all the dragons imprisoned at DIC and Jacob who-knows-where. I have no right to be having fun while they're locked up for something I did. Sani notices my rapid shift in mood and it affects his own, so I tilt my head down and look up at him with false mockery in my eyes.

"You're not nervous, are you?" I say with a wicked grin.

"Chen Lung is a legend," he says. "Somalia, Korea, Afghanistan, Taiwan—even the Cairo job. Kitty, we study almost every job he ever did in Strategy. The U.S. would be a disaster today if it weren't for his genius."

"Yeah. Genius? Legend?" I can't stop the sadness from entering my eyes and it's worse because I know Sani will notice. He always notices. "Either way, he's just a cripple now. An old man peddling tea cures to white tourists who think he's a mystic."

My father was injured on the Cairo job in 1997, before I even learned to walk. Sure, he and my mom somehow managed to successfully complete the mission, but the cost was too high. All of his other admittedly horrendous injuries paled in comparison to his heart—ripped out and destroyed by a rogue dragon paid off by some terrorist sect.

Is a weredragon still a dragon if he can't change anymore? The question was too much for my father, who left DIC, saying he would be better off if the traitor had just killed him instead of cursing him to live out the rest of his life as a mere human. I think he forgets she would have killed him, if it hadn't been for Mom.

Sani doesn't seem to know how to respond, so we walk into the shop in silence.

A Chinese man who looks older than he is with a missing eye and deeply scarred face is behind the counter, staring at the back entrance, waiting for me to walk in. "Katherine?"

The world's oldest cash register still in operation partially hides him from view. Apothecary cabinets made of every kind of wood ever grown cover the fifteen-feet-high walls of the long, narrow shop, and the unmistakable scent of tea and herbs seeps into my skin. A few tiny tiled tables with wrought iron chairs are scattered near the entrance. The shop is about to close so there's no one else here.

He rolls his wheelchair out from behind the counter and moves slowly toward us, appraising Sani with a critical eye. The air in the shop is cool with the night air so a woven blanket covers his legs, disguising the fact they're missing from the knees down.

Though I seek my father's advice often, we don't exactly have an emotional relationship, so I have no idea why the gravity of the situation decides to drown me at that moment.

"Oh Dad!" I fall to my knees in front of his wheelchair and wrap my arms around his thin, formerly powerful shoulders. I feel the stinging in my eyes that makes me wish for tears. I've now cried more in the past two days than I have since I was potty trained. When I finally get a hold of myself and pull away, he holds up one finger, indicating I should wait to speak. He knows something's wrong.

"African," he addresses Sani. I've almost forgotten he's here and when I turn around to introduce him, I realize his mouth is hanging slightly open. I motion for him to shut it. He shakes off the surprise of meeting his decrepit hero and offers my father a small smile.

"Bulisani Mathe," he says. "It's a true honor to meet you, Commander Lung."

"Chen, please. I haven't commanded anything for a long time." My father shrugs a little as he puts water on the heater to boil. "Do me a favor, son, and lock up the front."

Sani instantly obeys and my father adds lavender, chamomile, wood betony, and lemon balm—calming ingredients—to his signature tea mixture. I close my eyes and inhale like my life depends on it.

"Sani's heart is injured," I say.

My father nods and mixes up a smaller batch of lychee and plum tea.

As he prepares the tea, we tell him about the events of the last twenty-four hours. He listens silently, never interrupting with a question or comment. We finish and he sits there, his eye closed, teacup in his hand, thinking. Planning. It's what he's known for, after all.

"Your mother's at the D.I.C.?" It doesn't surprise me that this is the first question he asks. Leaving DIC was a complicated decision for him; my mother and I had been pretty much the only things keeping him there. In the end, it wasn't enough.

I nod. He allows this to soak in for a moment, and I let him.

"You shouldn't have come here," my dad says. "If they're looking for you, it won't be long before they find out about this place."

My mouth opens to defend myself, but I hold back whatever knee-jerk response was about to spill out. He's right, of course.

I hang my head and stare into my lap. "I wasn't thinking." Really, I was thinking, but only about how comforting it would be to go somewhere familiar in all this chaos. I wanted my dad, the most effective military strategist of all time, to tell me what I should do. The tea shop has been a safe place for as long as I can remember. Why didn't it occur to me that was no longer the case? I glance at Sani and find my feelings mirrored in his face. I shake my head at myself as I realize that confronting Gesina at her house had been the same kind of stupid, too. I need to be smarter if I'm going to make it through this mess and keep all of us alive. I need to live up to my family legacy. I need to think like a Lung.

"He's right, Kitty," Sani says softly. "We should go."

I know I've put us all in danger by coming here, but I still have questions that need to be answered. For a second, I want to ask my dad to come with us, but I know that's another stupid, emotional decision. He wouldn't go, anyway. He'd slow us down, and we all know it.

I try to sound as little like a scared child as possible and more like a commander asking her team for input. "We will. But since we're here, I'd like my dad's assessment of the situation."

My father nods. "You said this girl had a long, white, furry tail?" Though I expect it, there's not a touch of mockery or doubt in the question.

"That's what I think I saw."

"Did you see it?" my father asks Sani. The poor boy hasn't spoken much since we got here, star struck by my father's presence.

"No, sir," he says.

"Lose the 'sir,' boy," my father says. "I have no rank anymore."

"Yes si… um, okay." Sani swallows like it's as hard as bench-pressing his max. "I was shot. Unconscious when Gesina got away." He lowers his eyes to the swirling herbs in his tea and fiddles with his cup.

"There's no shame in taking a bullet for the mission, understand?"

"Two," I say.

"I'm sorry?" my dad asks.

"He took two bullets."

My father's gruff voice softens as he addresses Sani. "First mission failure?"

"Yes."

"It gets easier."

Those few words seem to have filled the hole inside Sani that his dragon-fast healing left behind. Satisfied, my father moves the conversation back to this afternoon's events.

"This girl. She was pretty?" he asks.

"Gorgeous," Sani says. Though I agree with him and I have no real right to feel this way, the word feels like a betrayal.

I feel acid burning my throat as I say, "Prettiest I've ever seen."

"Jacob seemed entranced by her? More than usual?"

A pang of guilt stabs through my gut as I remember him begging me to go with him this afternoon, to make *her* more comfortable. If I had gone with him, would things have turned out differently?

"I guess so," I say. "He's pretty girl-crazy, though, so it'd be hard to tell."

"And you were confused when she touched you?" he asks.

I cross my arms and narrow my eyes at him. "That's what I said. What's going on? You know something, don't you? Tell me."

"Kitsune," he says. The word lingers in the air, ominous and slightly terrifying. Like I'm supposed to know what that means.

"No way." Sani forgets his reverence and fear of my father. "They're a myth."

A sharp sound that I'm pretty sure is a laugh escapes my father's torn lips. "You're a *dragon*."

"Point taken," Sani says, slouching his shoulders.

"Um, somebody want to fill me in?" I ask.

"Japanese fox spirits," Sani says. "I don't know much about them. I only know the name because Wallace showed me an anime about them."

"Shapeshifters," my father says. "Except they're all female and can take any female shape, including your young Ambassador's daughter—and they're always beautiful—heartbreakingly beautiful. They can bewitch people by looking them in the eyes, make them do whatever they want."

"No," I say. "If she could do that, why wouldn't she do it *before* I tackled her?"

"Sounds like every time she did it to you, she touched you," Sani says. There's that eye—and ear—for details.

"Because you're a dragon, her ability isn't as strong on you," my father says.

"Oh, it's plenty strong," I say, remembering that ridiculous feeling of being lost in the woods in the middle of a crowd.

"Okay," Sani says. "Harder to activate, then." He gives me that don't-be-contrary look he has to use almost every day at school. Sometimes I think Sani's real assignment is to keep me in check.

Kitsune. I've never heard of such a thing. Wait a minute. Why haven't I heard anything about these monsters?

"Why do you know so much about them?" I ask my father, accusation dripping from my words. He sighs, and an old sadness floods his scarred face. Tears should be welling up in his eyes, but evolution has spared him that. He motions to his second heart—or where it should be.

"The rogue *dragon* who betrayed us and would have killed me if your mother hadn't disobeyed orders and come back for me—" He stops and actually *smiles*. It's a sad, regretful smile, but it's the first true smile I've seen from him in years. "She was magnificent, Kitty. Fierce, powerful, like an avenging angel."

"Dad," I gently say to bring him back to the issue at hand. It breaks my heart to disturb his reverie, but I need to know. "You're saying the woman who did this to you wasn't a dragon?"

"She was kitsune, a mercenary we paid to help us out with the mission."

"How could she betray you like that?" Sani says. The disgust is written plainly on his face, and I know he can't imagine turning on DIC after all we've done for him.

"Kitsune value many things and none of them are loyalty," my father says. "Someone offered her more money and a chance to cause chaos, so she went for it. She was the one who ended up paying, though, thanks to your mother."

This fox woman I never knew about almost blew the biggest mission DIC has ever attempted, maimed my father, and was killed by my mother. Anger wells up in me and burns my stomach until I want to spit fire. "You're saying DIC knew these things existed and they never bothered to tell us? My mom never told me? You—" and my voice cracks like a traitorous bastard. "You never told me."

"They're so secretive and slippery. We thought she was the last one," my father says. It's hard to read the emotions on his ruined face, but he sounds defensive. Still defending DIC and my mother.

"And the director was probably ashamed to admit he trusted one of these creatures," Sani says.

My father nods. There's one thing that still confuses me. "Why could I see her tail in the helicopter? The rest of her was human."

"Kitsune can't maintain complete control of the shift when they're flustered," my father says. "If they're injured or stressed, their tails will show. It's like when the dragon tries to take over when you're angry, but even harder to control. But with smaller consequences."

As long as you don't mind being outed as a mythological creature.

"Wait," Sani says. He would never do anything as undignified as a facepalm, but he looks like he wants to. "Fuchs."

"Huh?" I ask.

"It's German for 'fox.' We were trying to figure out why Gesina's last name was wrong." Realization crawls across his face. "She did it on purpose."

Sighing, my father says, "Kitsune like to play games with their prey. It's very possible she meant for you to figure it out."

I slap a hand on the table, rattling the teacups. "She was messing with us!"

My mind decides of its own accord to move past the pain of being lied to and manipulated and toward the plan on how to kick this fox's tail. How do I fight someone who can practically send me into a coma as soon as she touches me? That's an easy one, Kitty: don't touch her. "Weapons," I say. "I need weapons."

"For what?" my father says. He knows I'm not a fan of guns. On this subject, I'm more old-fashioned than he is.

"To get Jacob back." Duh.

"Katherine," my father says, his voice breaking. "I heard the news. The president is holding the dragons prisoner."

"And?"

"Your responsibility to him is breached," my father says. His tone is harsh and quiet, like polished steel. "Even if you rescue him—and I don't know how you will without any idea where he is—they'll only repay you by tossing you in with the others."

"Oh, good point," I say. I'd been on mission autopilot and hadn't even stopped to consider how one affected the other. Why rescue the son of the man who represents the country that's holding my mother and friends hostage?

Then, my conscience speaks up. His name is Sani. "Can you really abandon Jacob to that woman? Who knows what she wants with him? Right is still right, no matter how you're repaid."

After spending three years with that kind of honor, it's no wonder I lov—um, like him. I like him. A freaking lot.

"You don't owe them anything," my father says, his face reddening. "Your mother, your friends, they're all being held by—" He stops and tilts his head to the side like a dog listening to the wind. My father's special gift is amazing sensory perception, and he still accesses some of it, even in human form. His hearing and eyesight were once even better than the best African dragon.

"Someone's coming. Paramilitary. Armed," he says. He looks at me with a wide eye.

Chen Lung doesn't get scared. Everyone knows that. But he looks terrified right now.

"Hide," he whispers fiercely.

Sani grabs my arm and starts pulling me behind the counter.

"No," my father says. "*Hide.*"

"Right." I move to the most open part of the shop and allow my dragon self to completely take over. Even pulling my coils in as tightly as I can, I miscalculate, and the sudden increase in size knocks a teacup off the table. The cup falls to the cement floor and my enhanced dragon senses give me the distinct displeasure of hearing every crack form and break. Maybe the expression should be "dragon in a china shop."

Sani climbs on to my back and whispers, "Up."

Concentrating on not breaking anything else, I slowly increase my altitude until we hover just below the ceiling. Sani presses flat against me, wrapping his arms around my neck, and we disappear just as six serious-looking, seriously jacked men with coats that bulge in all the dangerous places walk in the front door. The door that had been locked. The hanging bell resonates into the sudden silence. Before the door slams shut, I see no fewer than four black government-issued SUVs and accompanying CIA thugs waiting out on the street.

"Mr. Chen?" the man in front asks. He's the oldest of them, with a cleft chin, splashes of gray in his dark, cropped hair, and the hint of an aging body hanging over his belt.

"Know anyone else who looks like this?" my father asks, some of the old fire still making him defiant. He sits tall and proud, not giving away a single thing.

"Do you know where your daughter is?" Cleft Chin gets straight to the point. He stares into my father's good eye unflinchingly—something very few people on the planet can accomplish—like he's going to read the answer there.

"Haven't seen her in months." If there's one thing all DIC operatives excel at, it's lying. I—the aforementioned daughter—was floating here and *I* believed him.

Cleft Chin stares hard at my father before letting his gaze slide across the room. It stops when he sees the two cups on the table and one shattered on the floor.

"Months?" Cleft Chin says. He turns to the five guys at his back. "Search the place."

They obey immediately, fanning out to different areas of the room, one going to the back storage area. Four of them pass directly underneath me so closely I feel the air disturbed by their movement. Both of my hearts erupt in a synchronized techno beat and Sani tightens his grip around my scaled neck, his hearts joining mine until I can't hear anything but crazed thumps. If they have heat sensors or particularly good hearing, we're screwed.

"Clear," a goon declares. He's soon echoed by all the others.

Cleft Chin swaggers closer to my father and bends over to look him eyes-to-eye. "Where's Katherine?"

The guy doesn't know it, but this is the second he makes his big mistake. Saying my full name lets my dad know this guy knows absolutely nothing about me except what my official file says. And my dad will give him no more.

My father's face stares back at him like a stone gargoyle, unmoving and hard. Liquid fire rises up in his eyes, begging for release, and my dragon-self aches to respond, but I sand-bag it with fear and restraint. Mostly fear, though.

"Search harder," Cleft Chin orders his men, his jaw clenching and unclenching.

Half a second after the command is given, the first crash rips through the air as an apothecary cabinet is knocked to the ground. Now there are so many things breaking and shattering I can't keep up with the sounds.

Broken shards of glass, fragments of teacups, and a shower of herbs assault my scales and fall to the floor, harmless. I turn to look at Sani, who has his eyes slammed shut. His grip on my neck would choke me if not for the thick scales.

A teacup thrown high bounces off my belly, and I hold my breath, wondering if any of them saw it change direction in mid-air. But it doesn't matter. The men aren't even attempting to look for me; they're simply destroying the place.

Jackasses.

I clamp my jaws shut, knowing that reacting wouldn't help. Yesterday, my father was one of the most trusted and reliable consultants on covert strategy for the U.S. government. Today, he's worse than a criminal—not even allowed the basic rights of the Constitution he gave his life, legs, eye, heart, and family to protect.

And it's my freaking fault.

Watching this is different from a vague notion that the government is holding the dragons. Even the president's announcement and the warning from Wallace didn't solidify the betrayal, but every crash and break builds the picture in my mind like a computer rendering a scene, pixel by pixel.

As the thugs run out of things to break, the percussion slows and stops.

I know my father's dragon-self must be searing with rage, as mine is, but he doesn't show it. "Told you she wasn't here," he says simply.

"That's too bad," Cleft Chin says. He shrugs. "At least we'll be returning one rogue dragon to the compound."

One rogue dragon? I don't think there are any other dragons out on assignment today due to last night's mishap. Domestic missions had been immediately recalled, and foreign missions were told to hold off on returning until further notice was given. Who could they be bringing in?

When one of the thugs takes out a pair of handcuffs, I realize they're talking about my father. My dragon-self roars in my head, the sound drowning out all logical thought.

"No!" I yell, but only Sani can hear me. My ability protects us from being heard, though I'm ready to lose control of that when Sani places a hand on the side of my dragon-head.

"Kitty." He sounds scared, but far more in control than I am. "Look at me."

I can't. These assholes are putting handcuffs on my wheelchair-bound father and I'm calculating how many seconds it would take for me to rip out all of their throats. Less than three, I'd bet.

"Your father doesn't want you caught," he says. "They have half an army outside and I still can't change."

They start wheeling him out and the full length of my dragon body tenses. I'm thinking, as mad as I am, I could take out the bulk of the U.S. Army right now. If I let the dragon take full control, I probably wouldn't even feel bad about it. I loosen my hold on the magnetic currents keeping me aloft and we descend a few inches.

"Look at me." I hear Sani's plea on the very edge of my rage-colored world. "Damn it, Kitty!"

That, of all things, steals my attention. Sani doesn't cuss. Ever. I've seen him stabbed with a six-inch blade, fall seven stories down a climbing wall, and now shot—and he's never uttered so much as an "oh, poop."

I freeze our descent.

"Look at me," he says again.

I turn my head slowly and meet his eyes, the cool green tempering my frenzy just enough so I can think clearly again. He places both hands on either side of my snout now, and his fingers feel like ice against the heat of my temper. My dragon quiets, and I feel very much like a teenage girl again, thrilling at Sani's intimate touch.

"We'll get him back," he says. "I promise. But not now. There are too many of them outside. Listen, can you hear them?"

Closing my eyes, I let my hearing slide outside the shop's front door. The rustle of gunmetal on leather, car doors closing, footsteps. There are at least forty men out there. Crap.

Forty men to get an old cripple and a sixteen-year-old girl? That's a Public Enemy Number One situation.

Exhausted, I lower us to the littered ground. I stand there, Sani's hands on my dragon face, amid the rubble of a ruined Chinese tea shop, until we hear the last man get in a car and drive away.

I echo Sani's words. "We'll get him back."

Chapter Seven

I'm still in dragon form when we retreat to the storage area through the roll-up cargo door because my anger hasn't slackened enough for my dragon-self to release its hold. It's a weakness I seem to endure more than most other dragons; what does that say about me?

I raise my tail to move back the corner ceiling tile and lower the bag of handguns and grenades my father revealed to me when I was ten, "just in case." There really is no such thing as an ex-spook. I have no idea how he ever intended on reaching them himself, though — or how they got there in the first place. Sani unzips the bag and reveals a note laying on top. He picks it up.

"I can't read it," he says. "I think it's Chinese?" Sani speaks six languages, but not this one.

"Let me see." I only speak four fluently, but Chinese is one of them.

He holds it up for me. "Katherine," I translate and read

out loud. "I hope the time won't come when you'll need these, but I also fear you won't reach retirement before that time arrives. Wherever I am as you read this, know that I believe in you. Loyalty and justice, always."

Sadness overtakes me. And a little…amusement? My father, the master strategist, Gods bless him.

My dragon-self finally fades back inside me and, for the first time since I was a kid, the change overwhelms me. I stumble on my seemingly inadequate single pair of feet. Sani catches me in his arms, and I surrender to his strength until I regain my own.

My arms linger around his waist longer than necessary, and I search his eyes for something I've not found the other hundred times I've looked. His gaze is guarded, as usual.

As he takes in my face, though, something tender flickers deep in his eyes. Maybe it's wishful thinking.

"Hey," he murmurs. "Are you okay?"

"Oh yeah. I'm peachy." I try to maintain my carefully crafted tough-girl image, but my voice cracks. The truth is, I can't tell him I'm on the verge of falling apart. If I start down that road, it will drag us both into my turmoil, and nobody has time for that.

His fingers pulse where they rest on my back. "Kitty."

My name on his lips is a symphony. How can two simple beats of basic human language engulf me so completely? We stare at each other for a mini infinity. I'm terrified of speaking and breaking the spell that's fallen over us.

"It's been a terrible day. You've just watched the last of the people you love imprisoned." He stops, swallows, inhales a slow breath. "Whatever you need. I'm here."

My mouth forms words before my befuddled brain can

stop it. "He wasn't the last one."

Sani freezes and I realize my mistake.

"I mean..." I stumble, trying to find the words. "I have, you know, friends."

But we both know what I mean. If there was a trophy for moment-ruining, I'd win every year.

He pulls away, clears his throat, and begins to check out my father's bag of tricks. I'm grateful he's not looking at me because my face is probably blood-red with embarrassment. Look at me; about to start a war with the CIA on their own turf and somehow still a petulant girl upset about rejection from her crush. Pathetic.

"We should try to get a message to Wallace," he says.

"Yeah, sure." I agree, but that's about number two-hundred sixty-eight on my list of priorities right now.

We empty our backpacks of history books and three-ring binders and other useless props to make room for as many weapons as possible. Even distracted, I notice they're immaculate, like they were just cleaned last week. I have no idea how my father did this, but he's been known for pulling off the impossible.

Sani straps his backpack on and turns to me expectantly. "What's our next move?"

I freeze in the middle of putting my backpack on. "Me?"

Sani smiles sadly. "You're the highest-ranking uncompromised agent in the D.I.C."

"But I'm not a strategist! I don't..." I take a deep breath that rattles my ribs. "I can't."

"You have to." He's exuding complete confidence, but is it another facade? I've seen how good he is at lying.

I study my hands. My thoughts whirl so violently inside

my brain I can't catch hold of a single one for longer than five seconds. I can't be the one to make these decisions. I just can't. How did we get here? And what if we can't get everyone out of this mess? I shudder as I begin imagining what could happen to the dragons under the CIA's control. Maybe I've seen one too many alien autopsy videos. While I don't believe any of them were legitimate, the fear and curiosity that drives people to them is very real. From freak shows to Hitler, humans don't exactly have a great track record when it comes to facing people who are different.

"Try this." Sani's voice yanks me from my downward spiral. "Which should we focus on next? Finding Jacob or helping the dragons?"

He's right. I have to do something. Standing here imagining the worst isn't going to help anyone. I don't have enough information to make this decision. In fact, I don't have enough information, period. Solution: acquire more information.

"I'd like to have a look at the situation at DIC."

Sani smiles encouragingly. I can't tell if he's happy with my decision or just happy I made one at all.

"Let's ride," he says.

· · ·

Sani's arms wrap tightly around my neck just below my dragon-head. He usually rides farther back, but storm winds tear at us. The sunny weather from earlier has been wiped out completely by a storm that looks to be as big as the D.C. metro area. Sani and I have to yell at each other to be heard over the wind and occasional rumbles of thunder. Lucky for him, it hasn't started raining yet, but it's only a matter of time.

Lightning snakes down to connect with the earth a few miles in front of us, but it seems so much closer. The weird magnetic fields of the storm are already messing with my flight, and I struggle to keep the ride smooth. Sani's grip tightens.

"Last chance to get dropped off and hide somewhere dry!" I yell.

"Never!" he says, laughing. For a short second, I almost forget what's at stake. Sani's laugh, fierce and a little crazy, sends a thrill through me, mixing with the raw animal power that comes with flying. The wildness constantly knocking at my self-control flares up and screams in my brain.

"Then hold on!"

I push the magnetic fields around me until we're soaring as fast as I dare with Sani on my back. If I were visible from the ground, I'd probably look like a drunken lizard barely able to maintain altitude, let alone a straight path. DIC comes into view, and I realize we're flying straight into the heart of the storm. Lightning flashes every few seconds in the clouds in front of us, and the air hangs heavy with the impending downpour.

"Let's check out the gym door first," Sani says. Or he says something like that, at least. I can't hear too well with the wind crawling down my ears.

Circling above DIC, I don't see any indication of an occupation or invasion. As usual, there's not a hint of activity above the surface.

"Can you sense anything?" Sani asks.

"No," I answer, trying not to let my disappointment show

in my tone. I can't feel the emotions of a single dragon. Even worse, in human form, they can't sense me. Does anyone beside Wallace and my dad know I'm still free?

There is a large four-story training room on the upper levels that allows us to run drills in dragon form. It seems my kin aren't only being held in custody, they're being kept from shifting, too. It's cruel. And not too bright, if you ask me. I'm not sure the entire strength of the CIA is ready to deal with a herd of highly trained operatives, restless from not being allowed to stretch their dragons after a few days.

I swoop down to the tree line and slow my speed so I can dodge through the trees until we reach the manhole. Before I've stopped, Sani leaps to the ground and sprints to the manhole with two long strides. He crouches down and leans closer to listen, but freezes before he's close enough to hear anything. He runs his finger around the circumference of the opening and frowns.

Sani doesn't waste any time in running and leaping onto my back. I don't even have to make myself visible again so that he can find me, he just knows somehow.

"What's wrong?" I ask.

"It's welded shut."

Crap on a firecracker. There's only one option left, and I have a feeling it's going to suck quite a bit. "Let's see what's behind door number two, then."

The thunderclouds choose that second to open up. This is the kind of rain that feels like someone is dumping a big bucket over your head continuously. Sani wraps his arms tight around my neck and clasps his hands together below my head in preparation; wet scales are as slick as a used car salesman on a soaped-up Slip'N Slide. I take to the air and instantly feel him slipping. I start to swoop back to the ground, but he urges me on.

"Go ahead! I'm good." He wraps his legs around me, too, crossing his ankles to anchor himself even more. I try not to think about how his entire body is literally wrapped around mine, pressed as tightly to my skin as he can.

Heavy, fat raindrops pound my eyes until I squint as much as I can without flying into a tree or a building. We stay low to the ground and soar through the tunnel that leads to the covered parking area. As soon as we're under cover, I slow down so that Sani can relax his hold and wipe his eyes.

"You alr—" I start to ask.

"Shh!" he hushes me.

I shake my head to clear the water dripping down my face. Tanks stand guard in two rows, guns facing the entrance to the tunnel. About twenty armed military personnel are behind them, standing around, pacing, joking.

Joking. Laughing while they oppress an entire species. Chuckling as who-knows-what is being done to my family. Yeah. Hilarious.

A red haze filters over my vision. I swallow a growl that rumbles quietly in my belly.

"Let's get a closer look," Sani whispers. "Carefully."

The storm's insane magnetic fields are calmer in the tunnel, thanks to the thick concrete shielding. I stretch the length of my body out straight and hug the roof of the parking structure as I creep toward the small assembled army. These guys are prepared. I'm close enough to see that they all have a pistol on each hip plus the machine gun hanging from their shoulders, when a loud beeping sounds. One of the men runs to a monitor, and his eyes go wide, then frantically search the cavernous space. All I see is a red line on a field of green with yellow splotches.

"Confirmation?" a man barks. I almost lose hold on the magnetic fields when I realize who he is. CIA-grade asswipe Cleft Chin. AKA the guy who took my dad in.

"Heat signature confirmed," the slack-mouthed lackey says.

Heat signature?

I'm *this close* to diving in and swallowing Cleft Chin's head when he shouts, "Open fire! Open fire!"

Crap. *My* heat signature. Always with the freaking heat sensors. These guys are *really* prepared.

Thank the Gods I don't have to tell Sani to hold on this time. His body goes flat against mine, arms squeezing tight before I even have the presence of mind to bust a U-turn. Bullets chase us and whizz past my head. I press myself as close to the roof as I can without bumping Sani's head and curl the back half of my body to shield him completely. I could get hit a few times and survive, but if a bullet hits his other heart—I don't want to think about that now.

Thankfully, their guns don't also have heat sensors, otherwise we'd be dead meat. They have to guess at our exact position based on frantic glances at the monitor behind them. We burst out into the rain unscathed by lead. The full strength of the storm is centered over DIC now. Thunderbolts threaten to deafen me and lightning bolts race each other to the ground. I put us on a vertical path, fighting against the rain pushing down, to get out of range of the machine guns, in case the guards intend on chasing us.

The lightning flashing all around me is seriously messing with the magnetic fields now, but I manage to keep us aloft, if not super steady. Manipulating the fields is kind of like swimming, except I push against them with a magnetic force that I can work as easily as humans can work their hands and legs. Flying through the heart of a lightning storm feels the same as trying to swim through a riptide.

"That was close," I yell.

Sani doesn't respond. My hearts pound painfully. Did he catch a ricocheting bullet somehow? I have a moment of clarity and realize his arms and legs are still tight around me. And he's not the type to go into shock because of a silly little narrow escape into the storm of the century. I turn my head almost completely around to check on him. His head is cocked slightly and he's staring at the storm clouds.

"Do you hear that?" he says.

"You mean the crashing thunder and pounding rain?"

He shakes his head. I listen closely, trying to filter out the sounds of the storm.

Then I hear it. A whooshing sound with a fast buzzing underneath it. It's so, so familiar, but I can't quite put my finger on it. A very definite black spot appears among the dark gray clouds. The spot lengthens horizontally.

The puzzle pieces click into place and I get the full picture: fighter jet. Headed straight for us. It could be a coincidence, right? F-22 Raptors fly low through giant thunderstorms over major metropolitan areas in the middle of the night all the time. Right.

My illusions of a coincidence are shattered—by a missile flying straight at me. It would seem this guy has infrared, too. I mean, missiles? Really? Isn't that a bit overkill? I start flying away, but Sani stops me.

"Dive!"

"Dive? We'll be an easy target down there!"

"They're not going to shoot missiles at the D.I.C. with all of those CIA agents inside."

Well, he has a point there. And we both know I can't fly well enough to avoid the missiles without losing Sani.

I drop over DIC, staying well away from the opening of the parking tunnel just in case any of those CIA monkeys decide to bring a tank out against me. The missile whizzes above us, inches from my tail, and buries itself in a nearby hill. The whooshing sound gets louder as the jet prepares to make an overhead pass.

It turns out Sani's right—they won't shoot missiles at DIC. The Vulcan twenty millimeter cannon, on the other hand? I guess DIC is too far underground to worry about those. The rat-a-tat is occasionally drowned out by peals of thunder, but the bullets never stop raining down.

"The trees!" Sani yells.

I skim the ground, racing the Raptor to the trees. Closer to the ground, the Earth's magnetic fields are more stable than up in the clouds, so it's easier to maneuver. I hit the tree line just as the jet reaches us. A spray of bullets rips through the tree branches above. Some of the bullets make it through, sending up bursts of dirt and stone around me. I barrel roll, putting my body between Sani and the cannon. His grip stays strong, and he doesn't make a sound, which tells me he's okay.

I put on the magnetic brakes and huddle under the densest part of this mini-forest. The jet soars past us overhead. Trees aren't the best for covering heat signatures and the forest doesn't lead anywhere useful. Just miles of flat, open land in all directions. We have to get out of here, and faster would be better than slower.

"It's coming back," Sani says. "Can you outrun it?"

"Not with the lightning. Normally I'd be able to out-maneuver it, but the storm's mucking up my flying."

"What are our options?" Sani asks.

I have a feeling he knows what they are. He picked a fine time to help me develop leadership abilities. He knows I don't have any way to actually fight the jet, short of ramming it. An English dragon would be so much better-suited to this task. Too bad they're all locked up tight a few dozen yards below me.

"Option one: stay here until the jet banks on the odds and hits us both with that Gatling."

"I'd rather not." I can hear the frown in his voice.

"We could run. Hope we get lucky."

Sani drops to the ground and pulls rope out of his backpack. "Have you noticed anything about our luck today?" He starts tying the rope together in a confusing pattern of knots.

"What are you doing?"

"Your mother once told me a good agent makes his own luck."

"Care to elaborate?"

"We're going to run." He wraps a few coils of the rope around me, just above my front legs. "But we're not going to tuck our tails between our legs while we do it."

The shape of his rope contraption starts to look familiar. "That's a saddle!"

"Something like one, anyway." He looks unsure for a second. "You don't mind?"

I give my overactive brain a very strict order not to think

about the overtones related to Sani literally saddling me. I swallow hard. "No problem."

I drop invisibility to make his task easier. He can only see me if he's touching me directly, and he needs both hands to shape the rope. He finishes tying knots and lowers himself into the makeshift saddle/harness/thing. He pulls two semi-automatics from his bag, stuffs extra clips into his waistband, and straps the bag back on. A low growl sounds in my throat at seeing this side of Sani. He's the living embodiment of stealth and calm and—don't get me wrong—I like that. But this Rambo thing he has going on right now? With the torn, soaking wet shirt and a gun in each hand and that badass look on his face. Mmm.

The whoosh-buzz sound of the jet breaks me from my totally inappropriate thoughts. Take care of the life-and-death situation before continuing with the slobbering, Kitty.

I huff a big breath. Am I really about to take on the most effective fighter jet in the world in a lightning storm with two pistols for weapons? "Now or never."

Fifty feet to the east, the forest thins. I shoot straight into the air through the opening in the branches. I'm invisible again, but it doesn't matter. The pilot doesn't waste a second in laying on the trigger. I'm in between him and the city, so he's not going to shoot a missile from this angle. I try to fly in a corkscrew pattern, but the lightning flashes, and their resulting magnetic fields, make it more like the flight of a bee in the spring. A few shots ring out over my head, but there's not so much as a spark from the jet. And Sani is a great shot. Granted, I'm nearly blinded by the rain, even with the thick cornea of a dragon eye protecting me.

"We need to get closer!" Sani shouts.

Getting closer to a fighter jet trying to shoot me down has never exactly been on my to-do list. Sani's voice echoes in my head. *You have to.* I have to be a strategist. My dad, my mom, even Director Bean — I have to be all of them.

I swallow my reactionary instincts and think for a second. This jet has me outclassed and outgunned. I need to outsmart it if I'm going to survive. Shots dance around me as I swerve wildly in the air. My eyes zone in on the source of the bullets, the Vulcan cannon. One word resonates in my head: fixed. It can only shoot in front of the plane. Yeah, the plane can maneuver, but there's one place the heat sensors probably don't even go.

I go vertical. The jet is almost on us now. The bullets whiz by me as fast as the lightning crashing to the earth. Then a searing pain rips through my midsection. I drop dozens of feet before catching myself. White light flashes across my vision. I loose a roar that rivals the thunder crashing all around us.

"Kitty!" Sani places both hands on either side of my neck, guns still resting in his palms. They feel like hard chunks of ice against my scales. "You're hit."

My breath comes quick. Every pulse of my hearts sends pain shooting through my belly. My ascent slows but doesn't stop. "I'm okay! Let's finish this fast!"

The terrible burning pain in my midsection means the bullet has damaged a lot of muscle. That's the good news. Injured muscles hurt like hell but they heal easily and are less likely to kill me. As far as I can tell, no organs have been hit. I'll live. If I can escape this F-22 without getting hit again, that is.

I clench my jaw against the pain and circle up without

warning, aligning the length of my body with the top of the plane. Sani fires round after round down at the plane, but it doesn't have any effect. The bullets even bounce off the clear material covering the cockpit, barely leaving a scratch. The pilot, realizing we're on top of him, and he can't shoot us like this, starts evasive maneuvers.

Blood drips from my wound and flies out behind me like a long red ribbon gently pulling my strength away from me. I can't keep up with the jet much longer.

"This isn't going to work!" Sani shouts. I think I feel his words vibrate through my back, more than hear them.

I scan the jet for weaknesses. How can we take this down with just a pistol? Not even Rambo himself could manage this.

Lightning flashes close to us and the smell of ozone fills my nostrils. Magnetic fields spasm around me. A weight pulls hard at my right side, sending me into a large-diameter barrel roll. I catch myself before falling too far and fight against it.

That gives me an idea. The jet weighs far more than I do, so a simple tackle would be difficult—and would probably kill both Sani and me in the process. But I don't have to knock him out of the sky to knock him down. I think. "Hold on tight!"

Sani presses his entire body against me, and I feel the ropes tighten. I pool every bit of energy I can muster and shoot straight into the clouds above us for about a hundred feet. Then I reverse direction without turning, my tail end aimed at the jet's right wing. I pull on the Earth's magnetic field as hard as I can. Air whistles in my ears. Sani closes his arms even tighter around me just before the lower half of my serpentine body slams into the middle of the jet's right wing.

A crash, very different from the thunder, rings out, punctuated by little snapping sounds. Those would be the bones in my tail and lower body breaking in half. I roar with pain.

The F-22 wrenches to the side. I dodge out of the way in case it starts rolling. But it doesn't. The pilot is beginning to regain control. I straighten my neck and clamp my jaws over the right wing. I don't have the energy left to pull against the fields again, so I simply let go of them. The combined weight of Sani and me pulls the Raptor back into a spin. With my front feet, I push away from the jet, which is now losing control. But I don't push fast enough. The tip of the left wing, swinging around, strikes my tail and sends me spinning, too.

I'm spiraling toward the ground. I can't tell if I'm dizzy from the spinning or the pain of my battle-worn body—or both.

"Kitty!" Sani shouts. He sounds woozy.

I might be able to survive this landing. Maybe. But Sani wouldn't. I have to stop the spinning, at least. With a burst of thought, I snatch onto a magnetic field like a plummeting person grabbing onto a tree growing out of the side of a cliff. We jerk against the force and stop spinning. Sani sighs. Lightning flashes next to us, and a bolt of pain rips through my body, mirroring it. Then my grasp slips, and we're falling again. But it's a straight-ish fall.

The ground is close enough that I can make out the shapes of trees and rock formations, even with my blurry vision. I dig deep and push out one last burst of magnetic control, fumbling for the curved lines of the fields. Something connects. Just before my vision goes black, the weight on my back disappears and I glimpse a sleek, dark shape leaping to the ground. Then, the world disappears.

Chapter Eight

A soft touch on my neck pulls me from unconsciousness. I have no desire to open my eyes yet, but I know it's Sani. I can smell him over the dank mold of wherever we are. Cold humidity clings to my scales, and the full length of my dragon body aches with ghosts of mostly healed injuries. Every soft sound echoes back from hundreds of surfaces in all directions. Rocks along the uneven ground jab me, forming newer bruises by the minute. I shift, trying to find a more comfortable position, but little stabs of pain make me groan and give up.

"Shh," Sani says, rubbing his hand gently over my neck. "Don't move yet."

The ground under my head is softer. I will my eyes open to see what it is but am rewarded with nothing but darkness.

Panic edges into my fuzzy brain. "Have I gone blind?"

Sani laughs and my pillow shakes. Holy crap, my head is on his lap. My giant, toothy, scaly head.

"I don't think so," he says. "It's very dark in here. Give it a few minutes."

My eyes dart wildly around, searching for a trace of light to focus on. Maybe it's my imagination, but I make out a soft glow coming from several yards in front of us. This promise that I haven't lost my eyesight, combined with the soothing stroke of Sani's hand on my neck, calms me enough so that I can switch back to my human form. I lift my head and let the dragon snap back inside me; she's tired and battered and needs a break. I try to sit up, but Sani softly presses his big hand against my shoulder and pulls me back to cuddle my head on his lap. His arm curls around the back of mine, his hand resting firmly on my waist. My pulse quickens, expediting blood to my aching body and spinning head.

I let out a slow breath. "Where are we?"

"A cave. We got lucky—the cave mouth was right next to where you slid to a stop. You lost invisibility as soon as you blacked out." His voice is weak and low.

My gaze shoots up to the source of his voice and I'm relieved to find I can more or less make out the outline of his head in the darkness.

"You dragged me in here?"

He grunts in the affirmative.

"But...I was in dragon form! How? Is your heart healed?"

"No. I stayed out there with you for a few hours, but then I spotted a few more planes flying overhead and I could only hope the cave would hide our heat signatures."

"Yeah, but...*how*?"

I feel him shrug. "Slowly. I had to shift parts of you one at a time. I couldn't leave you out there. And you weren't waking up." I know my muddled mind must invent the breaking of his voice. Along with the tightening of his arm around me. Yep, I definitely made that up.

I'm trying to imagine human Sani dragging my massive bulk into this cave when something he said hits me. "Wait. A few hours? How long have we been here?"

"It's ten thirty," he says.

I take deep, lingering breaths, knowing I have to move soon. The situation at DIC is worse than I expected. That was a full-scale lockdown with fighter jets for backup.

"Sani?" My voice is barely above a whisper. "What if they never let them go?"

He rubs my arm as he thinks. "Then we'll make them."

"How?" We're only two young dragons against the most advanced military force on the planet. I'm confident in my abilities, but *come on.*

Sani is quiet for far too long before his grip tightens on my arm and he presses me against him. "Shh. You need to rest."

We lay still for long enough that our breaths sync. Even with the rocks of the cave floor digging into my side, I never want to move. I focus entirely on memorizing the feel of Sani's arm around me: the warmth, the impossible combination of strength and comfort. As long as we don't move or speak, I can pretend that arm means more than comfort for a wounded partner and that our world isn't falling apart before our very eyes. I can pretend we're a normal human boy and girl drifting asleep in the arms of someone we care about. I let my eyes fall closed and grant myself just a few minutes more.

. . .

I'm strapping on my overstuffed pack, trying to figure out our next step, when the phone in my pocket rings. The phone owned and serviced by the United States Secret Service.

All the numbers that can call this phone are restricted, so I can't know who's on the other line. But since Jacob's in captivity and the president is busy enslaving my entire race, my money's on my contact.

I punch the green phone icon to answer the call. "You have some nerve," I say. "Whatever you want me to do, you know where to stick it."

"Miss Lung?" The voice on the other end is one I've only heard on TV and on internet videos making fun of him. I'd been to Jacob's house a few times, but his dad was never there.

"Yes, sir." I say the phrase out of habit and ingrained respect, but immediately wish I could slap the words out of the air. All I can think is how the president of the United States has the gall to call me hours after taking every member of my family and all my friends but Sani hostage.

"The president?" Sani mouths the question and I nod in response, pressing the button on the side of the phone to turn the speaker on.

"You're the only one who can help me." I don't believe his voice is capable of cracking until I hear it. He clears his throat. "The Director of the D.I.C. is missing, I'm having twenty hours of meetings a day, and my son has been kidnapped."

"You know who else has been kidnapped?" I can't even

control my anger when talking to The Most Powerful Man in the World. "Every damn person I know!"

I shake my head at Sani, letting him know I made the mistake on purpose. There's no reason for me to give away I know he's still free—or, especially, that he's with me.

"Miss Lung, you need to believe me; I had no control over that situation. Director Jackson has been itching to pull the D.I.C. under the CIA umbrella for a decade, and he made a move minutes after the Lebanese Embassy released that footage—a move I couldn't counter without losing control of the country."

Gods bless me, he sounds sincere. But if there's anyone who can out bullshit me, it's the most popular politician on the planet.

"So what?" I say. "You want me to risk my long scaly neck to rescue your family while you continue to hold everyone I care about in custody with no foreseeable end?"

"You care about Jacob, too." The president's voice is so soft Sani has to move closer to hear what he's saying. "We have narrowed down his location to one of five buildings, and we can't even get close to any of them without causing serious problems."

"We?" I ask. The president sighs. Gods, I'm a smartass and I can't help it. "You helped figure that out, huh? I bet you went out with the strike teams too and—"

"They've asked for the nuclear launch codes within forty-eight hours or he will be killed."

I shut up now. Because I get it. The president will never give those up. He can't, not even for his only son.

Jacob will die.

"Miss Lung?"

I don't answer for a minute, half wanting him to have to wait, the other half dumbstruck by this situation we're all in.

"Kitty," I finally say. "Miss Lung is my mother."

"Okay," he says, like he's afraid I'll snap at him again. "Kitty."

I push aside the anger and the guilt and everything else, stripping the issue down to the bare bones. I have no idea how to help the dragons, but the president is giving me the opportunity to help Jacob. I have a chance to help the son of the man who's running the country that's keeping my family imprisoned. No, I tell myself, Jacob's not just the president's son. He's more. He's my friend. He doesn't deserve to die, no matter who his father is.

"The five locations. Where are they?" I wince. I know, somehow, I'm going to regret this.

"I can't tell you how much this—"

"Don't!" I say. "I'm doing this for Jacob, do you understand me? I couldn't give a flying crap about what anything means to *you* right now. Where are the five locations?"

"I can have my most trusted men meet you wherever you are with the information within fifteen minutes."

"Are you kidding?" I can't believe he would really think I'm that stupid. "Your *men* have been trying to get at me all day."

"Not my men!"

Good. He finally sounds mad. I know how to deal with mad. Heartbroken is so much more difficult.

"Either way," I say. "I'm not big on trusting anyone wearing a U.S. patch right now."

"Until a few hours ago, you wore a U.S. patch."

"So did my parents. And that turned out grand, didn't

it? Just give me the five locations, and I'll check them out."

"It's more complicated than that," he says.

"I'll make it easy for you. Give me the five locations now or I'm afraid I can't help you."

"All right." He sounds oddly triumphant. What is he up to? "The first is in McLean, Virginia."

Sani chokes and I try to cover the phone to muffle it. Is he serious? Goose bumps rise on my skin—and reptiles really aren't prone to such a thing. But there's not much else in McLean except for...

"You think they're holding him at the CIA headquarters?" I ask.

"I told you it was complicated. Want to hear the four other locations?" Cocky bastard. How can he gloat like this when his son is being held by psychopaths with access to a kitsune?

"All right," I say, giving in. "I'll meet *one* of your men. In a location I pick."

He pauses for a minute. I hear cloth shifting and a deep sigh. "That will do."

"The Reflecting Pool, far side of the Memorial. Eleven p.m.," I say. "If I see anyone else who even looks like another agent, I'm gone, and you'll have to beg your precious Secret Service to find him. Do not clear the area; I want the tourists there."

"I will send Agent Harris right away," he says. "Thank you."

"Mr. President?"

"Yes, Kitty?" He sounds hesitant.

"You owe me."

This time, he doesn't hesitate. "I know."

I snap the phone shut and meet Sani's anxious gaze.

"Trap?" he asks.

I bite hard on my bottom lip. "Maybe. The CIA kidnapping Jacob, though? Politician's lies are usually more believable than that." Though, if it *is* true, I'm not sure what I could do about it. I'd gladly take on the entire CIA to get Jacob back if I thought I could win, but that's an insane "if."

Sani pulls a gun from my pack and checks the chamber. "Eyes and ears open."

"Always."

Chapter Nine

I hover in invisible mode twenty feet above the designated meeting spot at 11:05 p.m. A guy, who I can only assume is the agent, stands there in jeans, a black sweatshirt, and a baseball cap, repeatedly checking his watch like a first-day newbie. Sani's on the ground, almost finished with his walk-around inspection of the square. It's a cool night so not too many people remain in the square: a few homeless guys trying to catch some winks on the benches before being disturbed by the cops, two stray tourists taking pictures of their reflections in the pool. He reaches the west end of the Reflecting Pool and kneels to tie his non-existent shoelaces—the all-clear signal. Even though Sani's the most observant person I've ever met, and he can walk through a crowd of the best-trained spooks in the world without being noticed, I hesitate. I'm taking a big chance here. As far as I know, we're the last two free dragons in the country. If this turns out to be some elaborate trap and we're caught, there's no one left to speak for us—because Gods know the president's not going to do it. He'll be too busy explaining to the American public how he could keep something like weredragons a secret.

Sani starts jogging southeast, looking back over his shoulder to see when I make my move. He slows and I know he's nervous that something's gone wrong. It's seeing this worry on his face that finally gives me the courage to move.

I swoop down and wrap my tail around Agent Harris's waist twice. It's necessary to give him a comfortable ride, but it will look exceedingly strange to anyone who happens to look up. My power only makes dragons I'm touching invisible, not humans, but anything surrounded by me won't be visible. Meaning, it will look like a man, cut in half, is soaring through the air.

I have to give the guy credit because, as I lift him from the ground, he doesn't let out so much as a squeak. Sani sees this and begins sprinting to the rendezvous location.

Once we've made a clean getaway and are far enough away from human ears, Agent Harris speaks. "Kitty, I'm guessing?"

I almost drop him when I recognize the voice. I catch his slipping body, perhaps a little too tightly.

He grunts.

I turn my head to look at him, to verify the identity I wish weren't true. I have to be sure. We're almost to the rendezvous location.

"Take off the hat," I say.

He fidgets, I'm sure due to hearing a teen girl's voice come from an invisible, scaly dragon. Or maybe it's just the talking dragon, in general.

"Now!" I half roar. The sound echoes off polished marble and rolls around the square like thunder. No one looks up.

Agent Harris slowly obeys me. The hat clutched to his chest, we fly by a streetlight, and yellow light flashes across his face. Agent Harris—Secret Service Agent *Dominic* Harris—stares back at me. He has minor burns on his hands and face from the explosion earlier today.

"Oh hell no," I say, dropping us both into my and Sani's rendezvous spot inside the Jefferson Memorial. I flatten my shape and we slip between two columns toward the center of the Memorial. I'm still six feet from the floor when I drop Dominic. I lower my claws to the marble and make myself visible, but I can't change into my human shape right now. Rage burns through every single vein in my long body.

"I thought the president said he was sending his most *trusted* agent!" I make my voice nonchalant with a sheer force of will. "Just curious; does the president need help with the definition of 'trust'?"

He mumbles a little, scratching his cheek and narrowing his eyes.

I hear footsteps outside and instinctively put myself between Dominic and where Sani will enter—half to protect Sani from the shock, half to protect Dominic from Sani. Worrying about Sani's approach allows me to calm down enough to become human again. He climbs between two columns and into the Memorial as easily and effortlessly as though he were stepping over a curb. As soon as he's on solid ground, he catches a glimpse of Dominic.

He really is so much faster than me.

Before I can even figure out how to react, he has the agent pinned to the hard floor, pressing his thighs down with his knees. His hands aren't on Dominic's neck, the way mine would be if it were me, but holding down his arms. I can feel his dragon-self trying to take over like the heat wave upon opening an oven. I'm thinking it's best not to intrude on this scene.

"I'm on your side, man!" Dominic says. His voice is brimming with panic and confusion.

I can see the conscious effort Sani makes to take a breath and calm his anger.

"You shot me!" he says.

"I did?"

"Twice."

He stares at Sani, drawing his eyebrows together; there's not a single trace of recognition on his face. Sani loosens his hold on the agent's arms, clearly thinking this guy may not be the enemy we thought he was. I'm not convinced. I saw him shoot at Sani until he crumpled to the asphalt.

"When?" Dominic asks.

"This afternoon."

Now he's really confused. His gaze scans Sani's entire body. "You don't look like a man who was shot this afternoon."

"I'm not a man," Sani reminds him. "I'm a dragon." The last word is punctuated by a growl, and it serves as a clear warning.

I expect Dominic to cower in fear, but he surprises me by looking straight into Sani's eyes. "I didn't shoot you."

"Uh, yeah," I interrupt. "I was there. You did."

Dominic stares at the ceiling, his eyes narrowed. "I don't remember…"

"Let's start with this," I say, pulling Sani off him. "What

exactly do you remember after approximately fifteen thirty this afternoon?"

Dominic rubs his arms where Sani's hands had been. They're red from the heat and pressure.

Through many painful starts and stops, we finally get our stories out. Either Dominic is the best liar on the planet, or he honestly doesn't remember anything after Gesina got in the car until she flew away. He claims it was a total black-out. I don't see a single tell, though he keeps glancing at Sani like he's a ticking bomb.

"I'm sorry," Dominic says, shaking his head. "I just found out about dragons less than an hour ago and that mere children were responsible for protecting Midday Sun at sch—"

"He has a name!" I interrupt. "He's a person, you know, not just a mission."

Dominic goes on like I didn't even say anything. "Now you're telling me there are shapeshifting fox women who can fuck with my head by looking at me and leave me with no memory of it afterward?"

I admonish him with a cluck of my tongue. "You really shouldn't use such language around mere *children*."

He ignores my dig. "How do I know you're not this fox woman pretending to be Kitty?"

I take a step closer to him and shift into my dragon form, roaring to accentuate my point, though the roar threatens to turn into a chuckle when he falls back on his butt.

"Right," he says.

I shift back to my petite, quiet-looking Asian girl form, giggling. Sani shoots me his very best stop-messing-around glare. He's leaning against the far wall, still trying to gain control of his dragon, not trusting himself to be close to the man who shot him a few hours ago. He stands in deep shadow with his arms crossed across his chest, making his biceps bunch enticingly beneath his T-shirt. My gaze trails across the curves of his muscles until he clears his throat.

"Fine," I mouth to him. I look Dominic over, assessing. "Give me your phone, tablet, watch, any other communication device you may have on you."

"I don't think that's necessary," the Secret Service agent says, placing a hand protectively on his left jeans pocket.

"Hmm." I tap my finger to my chin, pretending to think it over. "Well *I'm* the one the president begged to take this mission, and *you're* the one who shot my partner twice already today, and *I'm* the one whose entire race has been imprisoned, and *I* think it's necessary."

Dominic looks at Sani, hoping for some support. I think he's already figured out who the sensible one is, even despite Sani's initial reaction.

Sani grunts. "You shot me."

"I didn't mean to!"

"Agreed," I say with a devilish smile. "And we'd hate for you to 'not mean to' call the CIA and report our location or something."

Dominic pulls his phone out of his pocket and stares at it like it's a lifeline in a raging sea.

Sani pushes off the wall and steps toward us. "Look. The president trusts us—all of us," he says, moving his hand around to include Dominic in the circle of trust. I make a face at that.

"Including me," Dominic reiterates. "Meaning I should be able to keep my phone."

"However," Sani says, still moving toward Dominic. The

man's face falls. "The kitsune can look like any woman and make you do things by simply looking at you. On the other hand, she has to touch us to affect us—and all she can do is confuse us. I think, all things considered, it would be best if you can't make a call without our supervision."

I would say he snatches the phone from Dominic's hand, but the movement is too smooth and controlled to be called a snatch. He removes the battery with three deft maneuvers and slips the two parts into his jeans pocket.

I smile at the two of them. The smile is forced; through all of this, I've never forgotten we have less than two days to rescue Jacob—and let's not even mention DIC, my mother, my father…

Time for business. "What's the plan for Operation Rescue Jacob and Worry About the Rest Later?" Okay, so maybe I have trouble with being *all* business.

"I have the five probable locations memorized," Dominic says. He glances around the Jefferson Memorial with a skeptical look. I'd almost forgotten where we were. "Is there somewhere better we can go? Maybe somewhere with a map? Or some coffee, at the very least?"

What is it about this guy that makes everything he says piss me off?

"Well," I say. "We could go to the DIC planning ro—oh no, we can't, can we? How about my place? Oh yeah, that's kinda out of the question too. Hmm, Sani? What about your home?" I raise my eyebrow at him theatrically.

"Okay, okay. I get the point," Dominic says. He checks his watch. "Have you had dinner yet?"

Only then do I realize I'm starving. "I pick the place," I say.

"Of course you do," Dominic mumbles. I'm not sure if he meant for me to hear him or not, but I know a normal human probably wouldn't have been able to make out the words.

"This place?" he asks, at full volume this time. "It wouldn't happen to be on a train line, would it?"

A sharp laugh escapes Sani's mouth. "You'd have to knock Kitty unconscious to get her on one of those things. Enclosed spaces, limited exits, cameras everywhere, crowds crawling with unknowns."

Dominic turns to me. "A little paranoid?"

"Coming from a Secret Service agent, I consider that a compliment," I say, smiling. "No trains. And no probably bugged government vehicles either. We fly."

Dominic swallows hard as his eyes widen.

"What?" I ask, innocently twirling the purple stripe in my hair around my middle finger. "Don't trust me?"

"Can I ride with him?" Dominic points at Sani. I almost laugh. I must have really made an impression if he's begging to ride with the guy he shot earlier today.

"Silly Secret Service agent, African dragons can't fly." I don't feel the need to mention Sani can't yet change. "You'll both be riding with me."

"Let's go," I say, shooing them. "Outside. I don't want to try squeezing through these pillars with both of you on my back."

Dominic starts out first. I go to follow him, but Sani gently grabs my elbow and turns me to face him. My heart skips when I look into his concerned green eyes, and the soldier girl inside me wants to beat the girly girl inside me with a stick. I shush the former and revel in the way his gaze searches my face, careful and protective. Gods forgive me, I can't help myself. He pulls me closer, but not close enough.

"I've never seen you carry that much weight," he says, below Dominic's hearing threshold. "Are you strong enough?"

I shrug. "No time to waste, remember? Jacob has forty-six hours and dragon flight's the fastest. You know, I'm stronger than you give me credit for, Sani." I turn back around and hop in between two columns, hoping he doesn't realize I failed to answer his question.

I think I hear Sani say something. I think it's, "You have no idea how much I'd give you." But that can't be right. Now I'm hearing things.

Chapter Ten

I dropped Sani off about a mile back to pick up a map at a gas station. I know he can catch up with us in about a minute, and he was right—the weight of both him and Dominic would've had me sweating if dragons did that sort of thing. With Dominic still on my back, I drop behind the massive dumpster in the back of a 24-hour greasy spoon restaurant in one of the shadier suburbs around D.C. The agent is quick to jump off—I *may* have done a few unnecessary swoops and loops since dropping Sani off. So sue me.

I shift to my human form and round the dumpster toward the restaurant, narrowly avoiding the legs of a junkie who's decided this is a great place to pass out for the night. Leaning against the back wall of the restaurant is another scraggly guy staring straight at me, not seeing me. He's got a bottle in a brown paper bag in his left hand, and I can smell the stench of whiskey and vomit from twenty feet away. This place is perfect; there's no way a CIA agent or one of Cleft

Chin's goons will stop at this place for a bite. Under normal circumstances, there's no way I'd stop here.

There's a ninety-pound middle-aged woman sitting on the bench next to the front door. She's got an extinguished cigarette hanging from her painted lips and holes the size of my fist in her thigh-high stockings. "Are you lost, honey?" she drawls.

I don't slow my steps, but I don't speed up either. "No, ma'am."

"I'm no 'ma'am'," she says.

As a rule, I avoid eye contact with crazies. Dominic walks behind me, every muscle in his body poised to strike.

When my hand touches the door handle, the woman's bony hand wraps around my other arm. Dominic freezes. I look at her now. I know my skin is scorching hers, but she holds tight, her dilated eyes open wide.

"Are you some kind of demon?" she whispers.

"Ah," Dominic says. "So you two know each other, then."

I toss him a glare and return my gaze back to the woman. I see a couple of dime bags sticking out from her black lace bra. I notice the track marks on the arm still holding mine and the permanent dark circles under her eyes.

"Yes, ma'am, I am," I say, keeping my voice low and serious. "I'm not here for you tonight, but if you continue on this path, I'll be back for you real soon."

The heat of my skin finally overwhelms her deadened nerves, and she snaps her hand back, gasping. "Take me now," she says. "No use in waiting."

"Trust me," I say. "You don't want to go where I'm going."

With that, I turn and continue on into the restaurant. Dominic follows me, slack-jawed.

"What the hell was that?" he asks.

"Ever heard of scared straight? I'm like the supernatural version."

The waitress, whose apron is more stained than it isn't and who has more wrinkles than smooth skin, motions for us to take a seat anywhere. I make for a table in the back, close to the emergency exit.

"What gives you the right—"

"To save that woman's life?" I ask. Only when he leans over to pull his chair out do I notice the St. Christopher medal hanging around Dominic's neck. "Ah. You're Catholic."

"What does that have to do with anything?" he asks.

"What did I miss?" I didn't see Sani come in, but he's suddenly standing next to us, not even winded from the brisk pace he would have had to run to be here so soon. He has a U.S. map book wedged between his arm and his rib cage.

"Mephisto," I say.

"Ah," Sani says knowingly. "And Dominic's Catholic."

Makes total sense to him; don't know why the G-man can't figure it out. If I'm going to be mistaken for a demon, it might as well be the one who accidentally saved Faust's soul.

"What?" Dominic begins, but he seems to decide it's not worth the argument. He huffs out a breath.

Now that Sani's here, I scan the room. About six tables are occupied and no one looks out of place—except for us. At least four illegal handguns are stuffed in the waists of sagging pants around the room. No one would ever guess the two kids sitting in the back are the most dangerous things in the diner.

The waitress glances at us, but she isn't exactly in a hurry to get to the weirdo table. The walls were probably white once, but now I can't come up with any color besides "dingy." Weirdly, the floors are perfect, shiny light gray tiles without a speck of dirt or a single crack.

Sani places the map book on the table, but drops something else in front of me.

America's favorite adorkable actress winks at me from the cover of one of three gossip mags. Dominic glares at the magazines like they're infected, but I couldn't possibly care less what he thinks. Sani knows having this little bit of normalcy will keep me grounded. Sure, talking about who wore it better and knowing which thirty-something starlet had a bit of work done isn't going to fix anything, but I've always loved getting lost in the fantasy and glamor of it. When I'm reading about their disasters, for just a few minutes, I don't have to think about my own.

I grin at Sani. "My hero," I croon.

He nods, smiling a little, then motions for Dominic to begin. As I stuff my magazines in my backpack for later, the agent flips to California and points at one of the many inserts for Los Angeles. He spouts off an address that means nothing to either Sani or me.

"The rumored headquarters for the Yakuza's main warehouse?" Dominic says.

"Hold your horses," I say. Yeah, it's an old saying, but I like to be occasionally surprising. "You're telling me the first two locations are the CIA headquarters and a mob warehouse?"

A man with tattoos covering most of his skull turns to look at our table. Seeing the three of us, he shakes his head and turns back to his girl. She raises painted eyebrows at him and shrugs.

"It only gets more interesting from there," Dominic says.

The waitress finally saunters over, and Dominic closes the map. As if it says something that a million other maps don't also say.

"Drinks?" she asks.

Sani orders water and Dominic orders coffee, black. I glance at the grease-covered plastic cups stacked on the counter and ask, "Do you have anything that's prepackaged and sealed?"

The waitress stares at me blankly. Her dyed brown hair is pulled into a messy ponytail and she's wearing thick blue eye shadow.

"Something in a bottle or can? A carton even?"

"Chocolate milk," she says. It's not a question. If it was, I wouldn't have time to answer it, because she spins on her heel and heads for the kitchen.

"More interesting?" Sani prods Dominic.

"Possible location number three," he says, flipping to Virginia's map. He points at Norfolk. "PETA Headquarters."

"What the hell?" I ask. "Did your intelligence group just pick the most random collection of headquarters in the United States? Maybe they threw darts at a map? Oh, I know—the first five hits for conspiracy websites that popped up after Jacob was kidnapped."

"You know as well as I do that the CIA is the best at what they do." A harsh glint flashes in Dominic's eyes. "In fact, you know better than I do, don't you?"

The dragon roars in my head. My entire body itches to change. "You little fu-"

The table clangs against the floor when I surge to my feet, the sound reverberating through the diner. The only thing that keeps me from jumping across the table and causing this guy permanent damage is Sani's arms wrapped tightly around my arms and chest. We're standing in a strange, fierce embrace before I even realize he has me restrained.

"Shh," Sani whispers in my ear. I can feel his breath on my neck and, though it's as hot as steam, it sends a shiver down my back all the way to my toes. "Not here, Kitty. Not now."

He pulls his head up even with mine and indicates the diner with his eyes. I forcibly tear my gaze away from his face to check it out. Every single person in the room stares at us with differing degrees of annoyance. The biggest black man I've ever seen comes out from the kitchen and crosses arms the size of me over his ridiculous chest.

The giant is staring straight at me. "Problem? I don't allow no problems in my diner." His voice sounds like Mr. T gargled some boulders and washed it down with sand.

Sani drops his arms and returns to his seat. I follow his example.

"No, sir," I say.

"You sure?" he asks, indicating Dominic with a deadly glance.

"Sorry, sir," Dominic says, bumbling like an idiot. "Just made a bad joke about her mom. Won't happen again." It's the truth, more or less.

"See that it doesn't," the giant says, then returns to the kitchen without another word. I imagine that if we had looked like his usual clientele, we wouldn't have gotten off so easily. Only when the doors to the kitchen close again does the normal buzz of conversation return to the room.

Dominic unwraps the spotty silverware and refolds the

paper napkin before placing it in his lap. He doesn't look at me, but I'm pretty sure my eyes are burning holes in the top of his head.

Sani reaches under the table and takes my hand, squeezing it gently. Both my hearts beat so loudly I'm afraid the Unjolly Giant is going to come back out to figure out what the drums are banging for. I look at my partner and I forget about Dominic—hell, about the rest of the world. His hand envelops mine completely as I think he can't possibly know how this affects me. He's just trying to comfort a friend. To calm me enough so that I can complete the mission. That's it. Nothing more.

Get a freaking grip. I squeeze Sani's hand. No, Kitty—get a grip on yourself.

"The other two locations," I prod.

He tells us about a militant environmentalist cult holed up in the mountains in Colorado. They call themselves Justice for Earth and have made continuous threats on the president for years.

"And the last?" asks Sani.

Dominic flips to the Arkansas page, and his finger falls on an empty spot in the northern area of the state. He gives Sani a long, anxious look. "Zinc, Arkansas."

"It's not even on the map," Sani points out.

Dominic nods; he's stalling.

My right leg starts to shake with impatience. "And what would be there?"

"Let's just say I hope this isn't the one."

I growl under my breath. What could possibly be worse than CIA headquarters and the Yakuza?

Dominic leans toward the center of the table and gestures

at us. "I'm just saying, you two would not be welcome."

"We're well-practiced in going to places we're not welcome," I say.

Dominic shakes his head.

"Who is there?" Sani asks.

Dominic leans in even closer and glances around the diner. Even I, inches away from him, can barely hear what he says. "Knights of the KKK."

Sani's calm breaks for an eighth of a second, and he looks away, seeing a place he never wants to go again. This is the part of Sani's history we haven't discussed since he shared it with me a year ago: Before fleeing Uganda, he was forced to fight in an ethnic conflict he never truly understood. Someone else's intolerance had turned the most honorable boy I've ever met into an assassin at only ten years old. I don't realize his hand's still holding mine until he squeezes it so tightly it would injure me if I was human.

"Awesome." I allow some of the dragon's rage to slide into my eyes. "Let's go there first."

"There's no indication this is a more likely place than all the others."

"But how do we know for sure?" I ask, mischief in my voice. "Until we burn it to the ground and check?"

With a hard, slow blink and a jerky turn of his head, Sani joins us again. His shining eyes turn to me. "Not now, Kitty. We need to focus on getting Jacob back." Then, so, so quietly: "We'll deal with the rest later."

The swinging doors to the kitchen clang against the wall and Unjolly Giant lumbers out. He examines my face like a kid trying to memorize the periodic table.

A hush follows him through the dining room as he walks

to our table. Dominic gives him a quick smile. "Oh good! We haven't had the chance to order yet."

I don't know if the guy is just oblivious or if he's really good at pretending he doesn't know something's up.

The giant looks at me and nods like he's confirming something with himself. His sigh rattles the silverware on our table. He motions at the kitchen with his shiny shaved head. "Come with me."

My body kicks into ready mode. I feel the heat of Sani's dragon flare in response to a potential threat. I have no idea why this guy wants us to go to the back of the restaurant with him, and I'm not really planning on finding out.

"That's kind of you, sir," Dominic says, "but we really don't have time for a tour of the kitchen tonight."

"Wasn't even talking to you, son. And even if I was, that sound like a request?"

I'm ready to make a break for it, run as fast as I can out the door and down the street until I can't run any more — which, by the way, is a really long time. I stand up, and Sani's right behind me.

And so is everyone else in the room. I don't have to look at them. I hear the screech of chair legs against the linoleum floor, the rustle of clothing, and the less subtle sound of guns being drawn from waistbands. Safeties are clicked off in a gentle symphony. What the hell kind of restaurant is this?

Chef Giant turns around and makes his way—very slowly—back to the kitchen. He doesn't look back to make sure we're following him. It probably doesn't even cross his mind that we might not obey. I can't say I blame him with the amount of hardware in this place.

I shrug at Dominic, knowing I'm about to piss him off

and follow the big man. Sani is so silent that I only know he's following me because I can still feel his dragon straining to be released and calling out to mine in collusion. Dominic, on the other hand, could be detected by a deaf man.

"Give me my gun," Dominic whispers.

I shake my head.

"What if I need it?"

"What if Gesina—the kitsune, whoever she is—is back there?" I say.

I can tell by his breathing that he wants to object, but there's nothing left to say after that. I have a feeling he's flashing back to those lost moments from this morning, knowing I'm right.

"I'll keep you safe," Sani promises.

In a better mood, I would laugh. There's no way Dominic believes Sani, but he really does mean it.

Sani and I are both ready for action as soon as we enter the kitchen, but we're left disappointed on that front. The chef's the only one in the room, and he simply looks at a grease-coated TV balanced on top of an industrial fridge. The rest of the room is filled with flat grills, ovens, deep fryers, another fridge, and a soda machine. Down to the yellow-that-used-to-be-white walls, it looks like a normal grease bucket kitchen.

I'm staring at the chef, waiting for his next move. "Seriously, what's going on?"

"Shit!" Dominic says.

I don't look at him, determined to watch the giant chef as closely as possible. "What did I tell you about using that kind of language around *children?*" Yeah, I'm not letting that one go anytime soon.

"Um, Kitty…" Sani says. He's looking at the television. I'm the only one not looking at it now.

I turn reluctantly. "What is so—"

My yearbook photo. Words scrolling across the bottom: Wanted: Armed and dangerous. Exercise extreme caution. Do not approach. A phone number.

"Oh," I say. "OH!" So eloquent.

After the first wave of surprise, rage floods over me. We have a term for this in the clandestine trade: I've been burned. I will never be able to work undercover—if at all—again. I'm going nuts trying to save the president's son from an unknown enemy and the bastard's government *burns me*? Sixteen years old and my spy career is over.

Then I realize something else: it doesn't identify me as a dragon. They still don't want anyone to know one of us is free. I don't blame them. Dragons have always inspired strong reactions in humans. When I was young, my grandfather told me stories about villages who discovered a dragon hiding near them. Without fail, one of two scenarios always unfolded: either the humans decided to destroy the hideous beast or declared it a God and devoted themselves to worshiping the creature. Rumors of dragon-worshiping cults still take a turn on the rumor mill every year or so.

Sani, of course, recovers first. He strides to stand inches in front of the big man. "Did you call?"

He shakes his boulder-sized head. "Not a big fan of the fuzz and don't want them in my joint. You wouldn't be the first wanted fool I helped."

We probably shouldn't tell him what we all do for a living.

"And I figure a girl who orders chocolate milk can't really be all that dangerous." He takes one yard-long step to the grill and flips two burgers and three sandwiches over.

I don't correct him. I try to match his tough-guy devil-may-care attitude, but I'm afraid the shakiness in my voice will give me away. "So how's this play out?"

"You leave out the back door." He motions to a sticky-looking door to our left. "'Fore any of my other clients get the notion of reward money dancing in their heads."

He called them clients, not customers. Odd.

"Why are you helping us?" I can't figure out his angle—and I'm well-practiced in that little piece of applied psychology.

"Hey, gift horse," Dominic mutters. "Need a dental exam?"

Giant Chef gives him a look. I know that look. It's the exact one I'm giving Dominic at this moment. I choke down a smirk; Gods help me, I think I might like this guy.

"I jus' want you outta here before any feds catch on to your location." He speaks slowly, using heavy words. "My location. I don't want them in this building. You got me?"

"No problem," I say. "We owe you one."

I make my first step toward the door when my stomach growls. I can't help it; those burgers smell so good. Sani's head tilts slightly, and I know he's heard it.

"Any chance we owe you two and you give us those sandwiches?" he asks the big guy.

Giant Chef frowns.

"We're good people to have indebted to you," Sani hints. In a blur of motion, he snatches the three sandwiches off the grill, tosses them in a takeout bag and stands before the chef again before the giant can formulate a reply. Sani winks. It's not even aimed at me, and my heart clenches.

I shoo Sani and Dominic out the door ahead of me. Just before I shut the door, I turn to the giant chef, whose name I still don't know. He's already back at the grill, replacing the sandwiches. "Thank you."

He shrugs.

"Really," I say. "You have no idea how important this is." I can't tell him he's probably freed the last of an entire species. I can't tell him about Jacob. I'm not even sure he would care.

"Stop looking at me like I'm a hero, kid. I'm just try'na do what's best for mine. I'm not on your side."

"Got it."

My side? I'm not sure what side I'm on or who, besides Sani, is there with me. Heck, I don't even know how many sides there are and how they intersect. All I want is everyone I care about safe and free. It shouldn't be so complicated.

Chapter Eleven

As soon as I shut the door behind me, the phone in my pocket rings. We're near the dumpster and the passed out junkie. My hearts pound out a salsa rhythm. I fake a smirk. "Who could be calling at this time of night?"

The guys don't respond, so I flick the screen to answer the "unlisted" call. "I promise I'm working on it." I don't see any reason for polite hellos.

"Maybe you shouldn't work too hard," an unexpected voice says. Even though the voice is familiar, I take a few sputtering seconds to connect the dots. My body reflexively stands straighter, and my nerves sing like a violin string plucked by an untrained finger.

"Director Bean!" I finally manage to cry out.

Sani spins and stares at me, mouth open. I know my eyes are as wide as his, and I give him a tense shrug.

"You're not supposed to know this number," I say.

A weighted sigh answers me. "Do you honestly think I

got where I am without knowing a lot of things I wasn't sup-posed to?"

"How did you get it?" I ask.

"Not important, Lung," Bean says. "I hear the president has asked you to rescue Jacob from his captors."

My shock overrides a decade of discipline. "How the hell did you *hear* that?"

He ignores my question and my disrespect. "Don't do it."

"I…but…you…Jacob…" I can't seem to form a complete phrase, much less a sentence. Fluency in four languages and I'm tripping over my tongue like a two-year-old.

"You can consider it a direct order, if it makes you feel better."

An order? "Is DIC even…a *thing* anymore?" I ask, in-stead of what I want to, which is why he thinks he's in a position to give me orders. All of the dragons are impris-oned, and he's obviously running free with a network of in-formants just as strong as ever. The word "traitor" dances on my tongue, but I'm still terrified of incurring his wrath.

"Are you saying you're going to disobey an order?" Di-rector Bean completely ignores my question about the sta-tus of DIC. This doesn't escape my attention. Should I even keep calling him "Director"?

Sani's eyes are drilling into mine and, for once, it doesn't send thrills through my stomach because it's already tied into a thousand knots. Bean, the man who's essentially con-trolled my entire life, is telling me to defy the president, to desert my friend. I wish my mother were here. She'd know the right thing to do. Sani reaches for my hand, and his words from earlier sprint across my thoughts. *Right is still right.*

"I'm sorry, sir, but I can't just abandon Jacob."

Bean snorts. "You're not assigned to him anymore. The Secret Service has terminated your contract and cut all ties with dragons. Besides, you can't take on his captors alone."

I let the chaos that is my brain digest this information and toss it around for a few seconds. Director Bean is getting sloppy, and I only notice because it's something he's never been before. He has let me know three things: One, as much as he does know, he doesn't know everything—like I'm working with Sani or a Secret Service agent. Two, he doesn't want Jacob rescued. And he must believe I'm able to pull it off or he wouldn't make all this effort to dissuade me. Three, he knows at least something about the kidnappers to be able to say I can't handle them on my own.

I've never completely trusted Bean, but now I'm completely sure there's something more going on. Fishy doesn't even begin to cover it.

I know he sees me as a dumb, impulsive teenage girl so I decide to play that role like I'm going for an Oscar. I tend to play it pretty convincingly. I'm not sure what I base my decision on, but it's made. "He's not just my assignment…" I let the statement hang for a good five seconds and make sure to lock eyes with Sani. It's important he knows what I'm about to say is a total lie—not to mention looking at Sani will make what I'm about to say that much more convincing. He's still holding my hand and I squeeze it once. "I—I love him."

Sani continues to hold my gaze and my knees go weak at the duplicity of fallacy and truth in my words.

"Oh, Lord have mercy. Teenagers!" Director Bean roars. "That playboy? Do you honestly think he feels the same way? And what will happen if you pull it off? They'll lock you up and you'll never see him again."

And if I don't pull it off, I may never see another dragon ever again.

"Either way." I try to work the steel of my father's voice into my words. "I can't leave him to the mercy of that kit—" Sani stops me with a snap of his head. Holy crap, I almost gave away everything. Does Bean know about the kitsune? "Kidnapper." I hate this game. Every time I've lied before, it's been a script. I was playing a role. This is all me now, and I am no screenwriter.

"You shouldn't worry about him. The Secret Service will rescue him and everything will be fine."

They're strange words but they sound even stranger spoken like this. Forced, desperate.

"You're lying."

"No—" I hear a murmured voice in the background, but can't make out anything that's said.

"Can't you see I'm on the phone?" Director Bean scolds the interrupter. "Where's Mar—" He stops. I hear the slight *squish squish* of his mouth forming two syllables. My hearts are racing each other.

The person says something in a hushed, terrified whisper. I still can't make out any words.

"Do I look like a babysitter? Take care of it!"

"Marcy?" I say.

"What?" Director Bean asks. But I can tell he heard me. It's Interrogation 101. The suspect only says things like "what?" when they need to stall to come up with a cover story. Bean knows better, so he must be fumbling, rash and a little wild.

"Why were you just asking your crony about Marcy?"

If he escaped DIC before it was locked down, how and why did his assistant come with him?

A beat of silence lets me know he's about to lie to me. "I wasn't. I asked where Mark, the night guard, was."

"Don't lie to me!" I yell. Both Sani and Dominic look up and down the alley to make sure nobody heard me. The drunks passed out on the ground don't flinch. "Tell me what's going on. Why don't you want me to rescue Jacob? Why is Marcy with you? Where are you?"

"It's complicated," he says in the classic adult you're-too-young-to-understand voice. "Just lay low and I'll contact you when I've made it safe for you to come out of hiding."

"When *you*'ve made it safe for *me*? Like you've made it safe for my mother and father? The hell I will."

"Katherine."

He doesn't know it, but this is the worst thing he could say at this moment. Only my parents call me Katherine. My mother, who has trusted him with her life and ended up in captivity because of it. My father, who has served him unflinchingly for years and paid for it with his body, his freedom.

No.

"Katherine" doesn't belong to him.

No.

I don't belong to him.

No.

"No!" I yell into the phone. The dragon inside me hammers against the constraints of my self-control like a death row prisoner pleading for release. Every sliver of rage I've suppressed today comes back at once, weaving the strands together to form a cord of anger that wraps itself around my hearts and squeezes.

Dominic takes a shaky step away from me, but Sani is directly in front of me before either of my hearts can pound again. Just like in the tea shop, he places a hand on each side of my face. He's smarter than to speak so Bean can hear him, but his eyes are saying, *Come back to me. Stay with me.*

He's right. I'm closer to an involuntary change than I've been in a very long time. When we change voluntarily—when our human side is in control of it—it's a beautiful thing. A voluntary change is majesty and strength incarnate. But when it's involuntary? When we lose control and let the dragon take over? BOOM. Like a tornado let loose in a Tiffany museum. Like a bomb in a busy subway station. No one, nothing survives. This is where the legends of dragons as evil, angry creatures come from. It takes several dragons to subdue the crazed dragon and serious internal control to reverse the change. It's like trying to push the force of an atomic explosion back into the uranium. Many dragons never make it back.

Thinking of this only makes me angrier. Centuries of being forced into the shadows by a world that we've helped save hundreds of times. They should be bowing at our feet! Not hunting us like vermin.

I can't hear anything besides the roar in my head, the dragon's promise that it can take care of every problem I have—the kitsune, Dominic, Director Bean, the CIA. I have never wanted to let it run free more than I do in this instant.

Sani moves; I sense it more than see it. I realize the phone's not in my clenched fist anymore. "Kitty," he says. Just my name, over and over again, soft as lotus blossoms on his lips. It creates a tiny crack in my rage.

I call on every meditative technique I've studied since I was two years old. I close my eyes, try to picture an empty void. Nothing exists but my breath, moving in and out of my lungs. Except my rage seems to be hitching a ride on my breath, and my lungs pump it through the rest of my body. My eyes are on fire, and I snap them open.

Then I see Sani's worried face staring back at me. His hands are still on my face. They slide down to my shoulders, down my arms. His touch is ice sliding across my skin. He takes my hands in his own and shakes them slightly. The green of his eyes is a soothing balm slowly massaged into my soul. Even my dragon responds to his touch. I'm finally aware again of my deep ragged breaths, my clobbering hearts, every clenched muscle.

He pulls my hands behind him to wrap my arms around his waist and buries me in his arms. To be this close to a dragon who changes involuntarily is disaster. He's trusting me to control myself, to not destroy him. This, more than anything, brings me back to myself. I feel the fast, but regular, rise and fall of his chest beneath my cheek and focus on matching it with my own breaths. I have no idea how long we stay like this, the rhythm of his breath and the gentle pressure of his arms the only things that exist in my world.

Dominic finally finds the balls to speak. "What. The. Hell?"

I feel a rumble deep in my throat. Sani runs a hand over my hair. "Shhh." I don't know if he's talking to me or to Dominic.

The safety of his arms around me is like the sight of a U.S. Marine Corps helicopter in the jungles of Indonesia, like the first ray of sun after a long January night in Siberia. I want to stay leaning against him forever and let the world fall where it may around us.

Unfortunately, I know that having these thoughts means I'm diffused enough to get back to work. I pull away from him—slowly, because every molecule of my body urges me to return to his. He slides his hands down my arms until we're holding hands awkwardly, arms stretched out almost as far as they will go. He lets go, maintaining a gentle pressure on my fingertips for a few seconds after, just in case I need him again.

"Well?" Dominic broke the silence again. "What did Bean say?"

My gaze flickers back and forth between Dominic and Sani. They both have their heads tilted at a slight angle, waiting for my report.

I stomp down the alley toward the street. "I need to talk to Wallace."

"Wallace?" Sani says in disbelief. "That's impossible."

Two sets of footsteps scramble to catch up with me.

"Maybe not. I know a place... Well, it's probably better if you see it for yourself. I don't even know what to call it."

Chapter Twelve

All that time I spent training Wallace is finally about to pay off, but not exactly in a way anybody had planned. I didn't want to come here, but my options are limited at this point, and I can't make another move without some intelligence. Dominic hasn't asked an annoying question for seven whole minutes when we finally arrive at the edge of the warehouse district. Sani's head is on a permanent swivel. I'm not even sure exactly what he's looking out for. At this point, I've made so many enemies, I guess just about anyone could be out to get us.

I stare up at the imposing concrete-block buildings, biting my lip until the pain clears my thoughts.

I turn to Dominic. "Here's the deal: I can't make you invisible, so you either stay here—"

"No."

I take a deep, calming breath. Well, it's meant to be calming, anyway. It doesn't seem to have any effect. "Or take your chances with warehouse security guards and cameras."

He scoffs. "I think I can handle a rent-a-cop."

"Don't get cocky," I say. "When we get close to the tech warehouses, it gets pretty tight."

"Can't you just fly us in?" Sani whispers. His breath tickles my ear, and I close my eyes for a long second.

"No," I say.

Sani accepts this but—big surprise—Dominic has to ask, "Why not?"

"Lasers."

The agent snaps his gaze back and forth over the warehouses. He won't find them here. "Lasers?"

I shrug. "Lasers."

"Why do we have to go here again?" Dominic asks, a little healthy fear coloring his voice.

"I have to talk to Wallace and...well, the rest is hard to explain. You'll see." I look at Sani and ask, "Witnesses?"

He doesn't have to look or think; he's already assessed the street. "An ATM camera on that corner." He points to an intersection a block east. "That's it."

I usher the boys around a corner to put a building between me and the camera and finally let the dragon out, careful to control the change. Dominic jumps back at my sudden increase in size and presence. Sani wraps his hand gently around the tip of my tail, and we both go into stealth mode.

Sani could definitely sneak to the warehouse without the benefit of invisibility, but he doesn't know where we're going, so it's easier to follow me if he can see me.

Dominic, on the other hand, is so screwed. Oh well, I gave him the choice.

We make our painfully slow way toward the center of

the warehouse cluster. I constantly whisper directions to Dominic. He bumps into me or Sani more times than really seems accidental. Sani—the saint—mercifully takes Dominic's hand to guide him. Our pace quickens. Twenty minutes after we started, we reach the outside of the group of tech warehouses. This is where it gets complicated.

"Oh!" Dominic says. "Lasers. Got it."

"You weren't kidding," Sani adds.

I smirk. "Now Sani, you know I never kid."

He shakes his head and lets a tiny laugh escape. If I could make him smile every day, I could be happy. His eyes, through my dragon sight, are incredible. Like twin green flames dancing in the dark. Though, they pale in comparison to his eyes when he's a dragon: sparkling jade with more shades of green and gold than I could ever name.

Even Dominic's human eyesight can see the city dust floating in and out of the green lattice hovering in the air, connecting all the buildings from ground to roof, like a radioactive spider web the size of three city blocks. The windowless buildings tower over the three of us, dull and silent concrete facades with unknown electronic treasures inside.

I explain a little as they examine the laser system. "If you cross the plane of any of the lasers, a stampede of security guards will be here in less than a minute. The guards each patrol an assigned section of this area in a random pattern transmitted to them by the system. The guards have transmitters that tell the system where they are so any breached lasers don't make it go berserk."

"What is here that needs all this security?" Sani asks.

I shrug. "Something about gadget prototypes and software development."

"I thought all of that stuff was done in Silicon Valley and geniuses' basements. Why is it here?" Sani's forehead wrinkles as he tries to make sense of it.

My answer is simple. "Wallace is in D.C., so this is here." From what I gathered while we were training, computer geeks will do just about anything to work with Wallace, including following him around the country through his many not-so-legal enterprises. Wherever he is, is a mini Silicon Valley.

"How the hell are we getting through that?" Dominic asks, still staring at the psychedelic pattern of lasers.

"There's a single clear path to where we're going," I say. "Wallace can follow it with his eyes closed."

"Do you know it just as well?" Sani asks.

"He led me through it once, so…" I swallow a nervous lump in my throat and dig my claws into the asphalt. "Yeah, totally. I got this."

Three false starts later, we're finally on what I think—no, I know—is the right path. For the last ten minutes, I've had to completely flatten out to my full length and suck in my breath to avoid the lasers flirting with my scales. I'm about as comfortable as Shaq in coach on a transatlantic flight.

I'm stretching in a wider spot on the path when an armed security guard rounds a corner into the intersection we're standing in. The guard, a twenty-something man with gym-earned muscles and long brown hair pulled back in a ponytail, is grinning goofily at the cell phone screen in his hand, so he doesn't spot Dominic for a good five seconds.

His posture changes entirely when he realizes something is amiss, even before he moves his gaze from the screen. His shoulders pull back and his stomach stiffens, his gait becoming less steady. He begins to slide his eyes up and Sani is on him before his hand can reach the gun at his hip.

Sani's arms are so strong, but they still seem soft around the man's neck, his right hand pressed hard to his mouth. What feels like twenty minutes later, the guard goes limp and Sani controls his fall to the ground.

"Did you kill him?" Dominic whispers. Why the hell does he decide to whisper *now*?

Sani answers him with an are-you-kidding kind of look. "He should wake up in a few hours. Poor man will have a nasty headache, but he'll be fine."

Dominic nods as though he approves. As if Sani needs his approval. "Grab his security system sensor thing."

Sani nods and scans the security guard quickly. His hands are gentle when he slides it off the man's belt, like the man is a sleeping child he doesn't want to wake.

"Good call, Dominic," I say. "I may keep you around after all."

"I have my uses," he says, grinning. "They multiply when you give me a gun."

Well, I *had* been in a good mood for about three seconds. "I'm well aware of what kind of use you make of a gun, remember?" He can't see me, but the contempt in my voice is impossible to miss; I've been perfecting that for years.

His grin collapses like a neutron star. "You have to believe me, I really don't remember —"

"Remember what?" Sani has rejoined us with the sensor in his hand.

I start toward the warehouse, taking a more direct route now that we have the high-tech hall pass. "Let's get moving. Eventually they'll figure out Fabio over there is compromised, and we want to be safe inside the most secure building in this dump before they do."

We move silently for the next ten minutes, more quickly, but also more cautiously than before. I'm invisible again because even though the lasers can't see us, there's no such luck with the cameras. And I'm a wanted woman now. A few buildings over from our final destination, I find the now very narrow laser-free path and tell Sani to toss the sensor in a dumpster.

"You sure?" Sani asks. "Won't it be easier to keep it with us?"

"She's right," Dominic chimes in. I nearly fall over from the shock of him agreeing with me. "If the device tracks our location and security finds the guy we lifted it from, they'll know exactly where to find us."

"Kitty," Sani whispers at an almost sub-vocal level. He pulls on my tail to stop me, lets go of Dominic's hand, and places a long finger over his lips.

If it were anyone else, I might be offended. But Sani doesn't ever shush me just to shut me up. He's heard something. I hold my breath and stretch out my hearing. We're against a four-story red brick warehouse next to the bank of dumpsters. I hear it then: lazy footsteps coming from around the corner to the left of us. My heart races, but I relax. Yes, someone's coming this way, but they're not looking for us.

Sani puts his lips a hair's breadth from Dominic's ear and whispers as quietly as possible. "In the dumpster. Now."

I can tell Dominic wants to argue, but I think he's already learned to trust my partner's judgment. If Sani is being this quiet, there's a darn good reason. Sani kneels and cups his hand together and gives Dominic a leg up. The agent ducks down amidst the plaster, piping, and other construction debris, quiet as a mouse. Sani jogs silently back to me and finds the nervously flicking tip of my tail again as easily as if he could see it.

The footsteps continue their apathetic pace, maybe twenty feet around the corner. I take four deep breaths, then hold my breath. This is the first time I've focused solely on the sounds around me. Other than the footsteps, there's no sound of anything living. Air conditioners breathe, piping pulses like a heartbeat, and unimaginable electronics hum underneath it all, but there are no human or animal sounds for as far as I can hear.

My eyes go to the spot at the corner just as the footsteps materialize into a man. Or maybe it's a boy. He's wearing jeans, cheap tennis shoes, a T-shirt, and a particularly ugly jacket. Greasy brown curls hang over his eyes, which are glued to a tablet, where he's furiously typing at a virtual keyboard with all five fingers of one hand. Humans and their mobile screens, honestly. His feet follow the laser-free path toward us like they don't need the rest of the body's help. It reminds me so much of the way Wallace strolled through here months ago. I guess if someone walks the path often enough, it becomes second nature.

He's ten feet away, then five. Four. Three. Two.

The toe of his right sneaker barely brushes my front claw, which is attempting to make indentations in the asphalt. I press my full serpentine length against the cool bricks of the building. My hearts erupt. Sani's hand squeezes my tail just a teensy bit harder.

But tablet boy simply swings his leg a little oddly, like he's kicking at a rock on the sidewalk. His fingers never stop dancing on the screen. He walks past me, then past Sani.

Just as he approaches the dumpster, a rustling sound drifts out from where Dominic is hiding. It sounds like rocks wrapped in cloth falling over each other but, in the silence, it might as well be a thunderclap. I swear I can't tell if he's trying to sabotage us or if he really is that inept.

The only parts of me moving are my hearts. And I think they're attempting to make up for the rest of my body.

My mouth drops open when tablet boy doesn't even glance up. The *tap tap tapping* on his tablet screen doesn't miss a single beat.

All three of us might as well be statues for the next five minutes.

Chapter Thirteen

Dominic moves first. He clambers out of the dumpster, but neither Sani nor I make a move to help him. He brings a stench of stale garbage out with him.

"You couldn't be quiet for two seconds?" I hiss.

"I got a cramp." Dominic shrugs. "Didn't matter anyway. A herd of elephants could have run around that kid and he wouldn't have noticed."

Sani, face tense, drops the security sensor in the dumpster. "We were lucky. Let's not waste it."

I nod and lead the way. Finally, finally, finally we make it to the door of Wallace's warehouse. It's a crappy, dented brown metal door with huge chunks of paint in a perpetual fall to the ground. Under the shelter of the door's overhang, I shake Sani loose and snap back to human form. I have to yank hard on the handle, because it's rusted half shut. My body jerks back when it finally gives, and Sani catches me, hands at my hips. I meet his cool green gaze over my shoulder, and he drops his hands as if he is human and my heat burns the skin of his hands.

But the door doesn't make a sound as it opens, because the battered appearance is just a facade. Every crumbling bit has been carefully placed to make sure nobody gives this place a second look. I motion for Sani and Dominic to follow me into the airplane-bathroom-sized room and Sani closes the door.

The guys scan the room with their eyebrows raised. It looks like a broom closet made out of brick—and not a particularly well-cared-for broom closet, at that.

I maneuver to the left wall and gently push on a brick with a jagged crack down the middle at eye level—well, it's at normal male adult eye level, not mine. The brick pieces silently disappear into the wall to reveal something like a camera lens, recessed slightly.

"Give me a boost?" I ask Sani.

His eyebrow pops up, so I point to my right eye and then to the scanner. Understanding washes the confusion from his face. His hands nearly wrap all the way around my waist, and he lifts me easily. The pressure of his long, slender fingers against my stomach is almost more than I can handle. I forget how to breathe as he holds me steady at eye level with the scanner, until it quietly dings. Sani lowers me gently to the ground, and his fingers slide slowly against my ribs as he pulls away, sending chills up and down my torso.

The wall slides cleanly away, and a rush of cold, dry air greets us. I step over the threshold and lights flicker, then steadily glow. The light doesn't come from light bulbs, but computer monitors—dozens of them spread around a cold steel-gray domed room the size of my high school gym.

"Welcome back, Kitty," a pleasant female British voice announces. I've always thought she sounded not quite motherly, but perhaps like an older sister.

Dominic ducks and turns. "Who's that?" His hand flies to his side, only to find his gun holster empty.

I ignore him and follow the script Wallace made me memorize. "Thanks, CINDY."

"You've brought guests," CINDY says.

I marvel at the way a computer works a question into the statement. It has more tact than most humans I know.

"I did," I answer. It's the only response that keeps CINDY from sounding a silent alarm and emergency shutdown. Any other answer, and it would take Wallace days to coax the systems back to life, not to mention bring the full force of the private security company to our exact location. "Keep an eye on the old guy," I add.

"Understood," CINDY answers.

"I'm twenty-nine!" Dominic objects.

"Well, you're about as stealthy as a drunken elephant," I say.

Dominic walks to the closest screen and reaches his hand out. Before he can touch anything, the screen goes black. He frowns. I laugh.

"Does the D.I.C. know about this?" Sani asks, spinning slowly to take everything in. Aside from the monitors, which form a broken circle around the room, servers stand in rows in the middle of the polished concrete floor. They hum and buzz and occasionally click like a sleeping electrical giant. I imagine I'd be impressed if I knew anything about computer hardware. The steel walls curve up into a smooth steel dome with no light fixtures. I inhale the plastic, metallic scent of computer hardware.

"I don't think so," I say, still laughing. "Wallace swore me to absolute secrecy. I thought he was nuts to be so paranoid, but it turns out…"

"Why would he tell you?" Sani asks.

I shrug. "We spent a lot of time together, and he trusted me. He wasn't allowed out of the compound without an escort during training, and I guess I was least likely to rat him out. He programmed CINDY to let me in on my own 'just in case.' Like he knew something was coming."

Dominic walks from terminal to terminal, screens turning off as he nears. "CINDY is protective. She's like the guardian of computer geek Wonderland."

"I told him he was the Wizard, deep in the heart of Oz," I say.

Dominic smirks. "Then you're a Munchkin."

"Ha, ha." I roll my eyes as I log in to one of the computers. "That makes you the Scarecrow, then. 'If I only had a brain.'"

To my surprise, the agent smirks and lets out a small breath that just might be a laugh.

"So what exactly did we come here for?" Sani asks, bringing us back to business.

"I need to talk to Wallace and make sure doing that doesn't give away our position. This is the only place I can currently walk into with access to a computer that will hide my position from the CIA." I hope, anyway.

Sani watches over my shoulder as I pull up Wallace's custom internet browser and type in a website address. He snorts and I have to laugh; Sani is so rarely caught by surprise.

Dominic glances at the screen. "Are you kidding? Myspace? Nobody uses Myspace anymore."

"I know. Wallace said that's why it's the best public way to get a hold of him. Government bots don't trawl them much anymore and the low traffic makes it that much easier for Wallace's to."

"With all this technology at hand," Sani gestures at the room, "he couldn't come up with a better way of covertly contacting him?"

I shrugged. "Something about keeping it stupid simple or whatever." I log in to my fake account and pull up Wallace's. "Here goes nothing."

I type: *Hey Number One. I made it to Oz. If you have time, I could use a little help with my phone. ~Unlucky* Yeah, Okay. Probably not the best secret message on a public forum, but it should work.

• • •

I realize I haven't blinked for the past two minutes while staring at the screen waiting for—well, I'm not sure exactly what I'm waiting for. My eyes are sticky and slow to reopen. But when they do, there's a nice surprise waiting for them: Wallace's and Simon's faces battling for space on the screen. Wallace's hair is a strategic mess, as always. Simon's brown eyes blink back at me under the glare of stylish black-rimmed glasses and a shadow of thick black hair hanging half in his face. They look…okay. I'm not sure what I was expecting, but I'm relieved they seem unharmed. Whichever idiot thought it was a good idea to put Simon, our top intelligence guy, and Wallace in the same room together needs to be fired.

"Kitty," Wallace's soft accent admonishes me. "Please

tell me you didn't just risk both of our arses for phone tech support."

"Not exactly," I say, smiling. "How'd you manage to get a hold of a webcam? Or, you know, the web?"

Simon chuckles. "We whined about how bored we were until the guard took a hundred dollars to let us 'play games' on his iPad for one day. He figured it was safe since the CIA turned the wifi off." He elbows Wallace. "It took Number One about thirty seconds to get us connected."

Wallace's gaze falls in a fit of modesty. "We've been connected for hours. One of CINDY's auxiliaries notified me of your post."

Sani leans over my shoulder. The press of his chest against my back shoots feelings through my body that I really shouldn't be distracted by when so much is on the line. Still, heat builds in my stomach and inches its way to my cheeks. A blush spreads across my entire face. I hope the webcam aimed at us has terrible resolution.

"Hey, guys," he says. They give him manly, terse nods in return. Guys.

"What do you need?" Wallace asks me.

"The guard comes in every now and then; we shouldn't take more time than we need," Simon explains.

I press my hands together, interlacing my fingers, and squeeze them closed until it hurts. When I was just four, my father taught me how a little bit of pain helps to clear the mind. I need to think as clearly as possible right now; I'm wading out into unknown, treacherous waters. How much should I tell them? What if the line is bugged somehow? I decide to take a play from Wallace's book: Keep it Simple for Stupid. Or whatever it was.

"I got a phone call from an unknown number," I say. "A number that probably has top of the line encryption and all that. Is there any way you can trace who it came from? Maybe even where?" I know—under normal operating circumstances—this would be a piece of cake for either Wallace or Simon—but now? All they have is an iPad and a dodgy internet connection. And I'm probably crippling them by not saying who I spoke to, but I know I have to give out as few details as possible. Wallace is the best in the computer business but, as my father used to say, there's always someone better.

The tension in my shoulders collapses, and I fall back against Sani when a grin breaks out on Wallace's face.

"Yeah, mate," he says. "CINDY can do that in her sleep. Just make sure she can access your phone via Bluetooth or wifi and ask her."

"Are you kidding?" I say, the breath coming out of me like air from a punctured balloon. "That easy?"

"Don't act so shocked," Wallace says. "I designed her myself, you know."

Dominic speaks up for the first time since Wallace and Simon appeared. "Well, that was…anticlimactic."

Wallace and Simon exchange frantic glances. "Who's the suit?" Simon asks.

"Uh… He's… Well, you see…" *Oh Kitty, you are so freaking eloquent.*

"He's a friend." Sani uses that voice he has that makes anyone believe whatever he says.

"Right." Wallace's eyes track Dominic as he moves around the room.

"Don't worry, Wallace," I say. "CINDY's got him on a

leash."

The British dragon's posture relaxes. The blowhard trusts a computer more than he trusts me!

Simon glances behind him and to the left. "We really should get off here."

"Unless there's anything else you need," Wallace adds. For the first time, a trace of nervousness flicks across both men's faces.

"What's it like inside?" Sani asks. "Have you heard anything?"

"Nada," Simon says. "They're not telling us a single thing except that this is all for our own benefit and safety."

"And they're buttoned up even when they think we're not listening." Wallace's grin from earlier is gone, replaced by a tight line with lips pressed together. "They don't let more than three of us in any room at the same time."

"Thanks, guys," I say. "I'll put a line out if I need anything else. Keep your eyes and ears open."

"Will do," they both say, in sync. Soul mates.

I want to ask about my parents. I know they're only two of several hundred being held prisoner, and I should focus on the mission, but I can't help myself. "And if you see them…" Impossible-to-shed tears choke my throat, and I trail off.

Wallace nods slowly. "I'll make sure to tell your parents you're okay." He pauses, swallows hard, like he's unsure if he should say something.

Simon isn't so sensitive. "They're spending all of their time together in here. Attached at the hip. Commander Lung uses his condition as an excuse, says she needs to take care of him, but we all know the old man is more than capable.

Don't tell them I said this, but it's actually kind of adorable."

"At least something good has come of this."

I can hear the sweet smile in Sani's voice. It fills my heart with bittersweetness, overflows and fills my other heart and threatens to spill out of me.

As always when this kind of emotion threatens my calm, I return to protocol. My posture straightens and I raise my head. "Thank you, agents."

"No problem," Simon says.

Wallace nods. "Good hunting. Oh, CINDY? Override all protocols. Give Agent Lung access to all of your programs and capabilities."

A chill runs through me at his words. She was holding back?

I flick my phone's screen a few times to turn on the Bluetooth. "Wallace says you can do this in a snap."

CINDY's voice fills the room, coming from nowhere and everywhere. "Well, it will take some time."

Sani meets my eyes, his own filled with concern. It's already one in the morning. "How much time?" he asks.

"At least five, maybe six minutes," comes her reply.

All three of the organic life-forms in the room erupt with laughter. It's the first time since before the Lebanese embassy that I've laughed freely, without a trace of irony or sarcasm. Sani's eyes squint and crinkle with his laughter, and they meet mine, holding them there as though there's a physical force keeping our gazes locked. It heals me through and through.

We pass the next five minutes with circular talk about what we should do next. We don't agree on a single thing. Five locations, none more likely than the others. When CINDY interrupts us with her cheerful but bland voice, I think we're further from a plan than we were before we started.

"I have your results."

It's too simple and insipid a phrase to make my hearts explode against my ribs, but that's what happens, just the same.

"What'd you find?" I ask.

Sani moves to stand next to me, and we both end up staring at the same arbitrary spot on the domed ceiling. The heat radiating off him is a comfort, and I feel like I could survive anything as long as he's standing next to me.

"The phone is not registered to anyone," CINDY says matter-of-factly.

Dominic, Sani, and I all speak at the same time, something to the effect of, "What? How? Huh?"

"I was able to retrieve the phone number, but it is not and has never been assigned by any carrier or to any person."

My brain rattles inside my skull trying to figure out how a computer could possibly say something so illogical. How can you find a phone number that has never existed? Trying to understand this is like a dog chasing its own tail while running down a Mobius strip.

"What's the phone number?" Sani asks, voice calm. He's obviously processing this impossible information better than I am.

"555-264-8736."

Sani writes it down. "We could try to call it, maybe?"

His voice doesn't sound so sure now, and his forehead is creased with confusion and worry. We're all grasping at straws here.

"Would you like to know where the call was made?"

CINDY asks.

"Oh, darling," Dominic says. "You buried the lead."

I bounce on my toes. "Yes, CINDY. Definitely yes." I'm not sure how accurate she can get with all the protections that are probably on the director's phone—I mean, he was able to make it look like the phone number itself had never existed, after all—but if we could just narrow it down by state, at least it would be somewhere to start.

A map of the US appears on the computer screen closest to us. "I was only able to narrow it down to a one mile radius due to all the satellites that bounced the signal around."

The sound I make is somewhere between a choke and a laugh. "Only?" I'm pretty sure CINDY is my new BFF.

The screen zooms toward the west coast. California. Los Angeles. A square of L.A. city streets that looks eerily familiar.

Three human—okay, humanoid—mouths drop open in unison. I shake my head like a Magic 8 Ball as if the picture might change to something less crazy, but it's still there. The same L.A. city block Dominic pointed to in the cafe: the U.S. home base of the Yakuza mob.

"Are you kidding?" I scream at the ceiling.

"I don't kid," CINDY says.

I snap my head around and look at Dominic accusingly. "Please tell me this is some kind of joke you two are playing on me."

He shakes his head. He looks just as dumbstruck as I feel. "She won't even let me check basketball scores."

My dragon roars as feelings of treachery flood my veins. The pieces are falling together, creating a terrible picture neither of us is prepared to face. Director Bean called me from within the Yakuza home base to dissuade me from rescuing the boy they kidnapped. It all makes sense, but my brain can't accept it as truth.

Sani continues to stare at the screen like he doesn't fully see it, like he can't make sense of the lines and colors on the screen. He takes a step closer to it and stumbles. I don't believe it.

Sani. Stumbles. Just the thought of it is enough to silence my dragon.

The most graceful and stealthy being on the planet just tripped over his own feet. His eyes are unfocused, and his hands shake. I don't need to be able to sense his emotions to know what he's feeling. Betrayal. An emotion so devastating it changes every part of you, causes irreparable damage. Faith isn't shaken, it's shattered. Atomized. Especially the second time around.

Seeing Sani stumble and lose control of his body isn't the worst part. I'm absolutely terrified by what I don't sense. His dragon is silent. No roaring in rage, no calling out to mine for retribution. Nothing. He's not angry. I would gladly help him through an uncontrolled change one thousand times if I didn't have to see this.

"Well, I guess it makes sense, after all," Dominic says. "Kitsune are Japanese, Yakuza are Japanese." He makes a balancing motion with his hands.

"It *doesn't* make sense!" I yell. "That Director Bean would work with the Yakuza and a kitsune to kidnap the president's son? In what world does *that* make sense?" I've never completely trusted Bean, but is he really capable of something like this? He knew more about my assignment than anyone outside of my Secret Service contact, but why would he do this?

"I mean, strategically—" I cut the agent off with a glare that would wither a cactus.

I turn to Sani and take a single step toward him. "Sani?" I say softly. I'm scared, I don't mind admitting it. I'm not prepared to deal with this. I'm not a counselor, damn it. I'm a spy and a soldier; that's all I know how to do. So yeah, that's what I'm going to do right now.

"CINDY?" I say.

"Is your boyfriend okay, Kitty?" CINDY asks. "I'm picking up some strange fluctuations in his vitals."

I ignore CINDY's creepily insightful evaluation of our relationship and look at him, frozen to the spot, his dragon still silent. "He'll be okay." It's not a statement, it's a wish. A prayer to the Gods, to his God, to my ancestors, to anyone who'll listen.

I force my gaze away from him and back to the map of L.A. "Can you find the address for the Yakuza headquarters?"

An address and the picture of a huge warehouse appear on the screen next to the one I'm staring at before I've even finished the word "headquarters." I pull air into my lungs until they feel like they might burst if someone pokes me. The air spills out slowly, taking its time on its journey back into the world.

I have no idea what CINDY's capable of. It's time to test her limits. "Blueprints?"

The screen to the left lights up and digital pages flip on the screen, tiling as they're pulled from the ether.

I cross my fingers for the next request. "Satellite?"

"One moment," she says, like I just asked her for a tissue. Thirty seconds later, a live aerial view of the building in the picture pops up on another screen. Even if the picture wasn't fuzzy, I wouldn't be able to see too much, but there are definitely a few dark spots moving on the roof and loitering on the streets around it.

I walk over to the screen with the blueprints and flick slowly through them. Basic warehouse construction, nothing too special. They probably keep all the cargo doors locked unless some kind of shipment is being unloaded, so I won't be able to go in in dragon form. There are only three of us, but I'm confident we can do it. They're just a human crime syndicate, after all. And maybe a kitsune who can instantly immobilize all of us. And probably the leader of the (until recently) most clandestine of all covert agencies. Piece of cake.

"What's the probability that Jacob is there?" Dominic asks.

"Ninety-six percent," Sani says. Joy rips violently through me at the sound of his voice. It's a little dull, but it's calculating and lucid. I glance at him and he nods once. He can do this.

"What's the plan?" Dominic asks. He may be annoying and clumsy, but—despite all the bad things I've said about him—I know the president wouldn't have sent him if he couldn't get the job done. He looks at me, waiting for my orders.

This is my team. *My* team. They'll follow me into hell if they have to. A team lead couldn't ask for more. As terrifying as it is, I have to take charge, and do it now.

"I've always wanted to see that Hollywood sign," I say. "Tomorrow, we fly to L.A."

Dominic's face pales to the color of bleached cotton.

"Fly?"

"Of course. We don't have time to drive."

He swallows hard. "Fly, as in, dragon-style?"

"It's not like Sani and I can go on a plane; the entire country is looking for me."

"I can go on a plane," he says. "Nobody's looking for me, and I get priority."

My eyes narrow at him. "No way I'm letting you out of my sight."

Sani gently puts a hand on my elbow and pulls me close. "You can't carry both of us the whole way."

"I can manage it, with frequent rests." I say, chewing my lip. I remember how tired I was just flying from the National Mall to a suburb. Stubbornness will only get me so far. "Maybe."

"Even if you could, you're going to need your strength when we get to L.A.," Sani says.

"But—" I start. Sani interrupts me.

"You're going to have to start trusting him sometime," he says.

"I'll be good," Dominic says. He holds up his right hand with three fingers pointing up, his thumb and pinkie touching in front of his palm. "Scout's honor."

I scowl at him. "I don't know what that means."

I jump when CINDY's cheerful voice cuts in on our tense conversation. "Shall I make the reservations?"

I look at Dominic; he's trying his best to look cooperative. Maybe it's genuine. CINDY has already figured out I'm going to give in, and that crazy computer chick knows everything. Sani's right, I have to trust him sometime. And hope the kitsune doesn't find him again. "Yeah, go ahead."

"Done," she says. "And where do you want to sleep

tonight?"

"I figured we'd just crash here." I look around. There's a single cot in the corner, but the rest of the cement floor doesn't look exactly comfy. The computer chairs are perfectly ergonomic, but still made for sitting, not sleeping. We could make do for one night, though.

"I don't have any beds, and you have a big day ahead of you. Plus there is an unusual amount of guard activity due to an unconscious guard who was just found," CINDY says. "I'll reserve you a three-room suite at the Peabody."

"I can't check in to a hotel at two in the morning," I say. "They'll recognize me."

"I chose the Peabody because it has an elevator that goes straight from the parking garage to the guest room floors," CINDY says. "The staff will never see you if Dominic checks in."

A shiver passes through me. CINDY's forethought and intuition is downright creepy. I can't help but imagine bowing down to our computer overlords in the near future. I'm so glad she's on our side.

"I don't know…" I say.

"Wallace is paying," CINDY says. Do I imagine the little bit of singsong in her voice? Surely I do.

"We don't need the Peabody, though. Isn't there a shady motel where no one asks questions that would work better?"

Can computers scoff? CINDY can. "Wallace would strip my wires if I used my systems to even glance at a place like that. Staff at a place like the Peabody are as discreet as humans can be. That's why Wallace always has me put up his guests there."

I sigh. Wallace has a small room identical to mine at

DIC, so it's easy to forget how loaded he is. "Okay, fine."

"Reservation is made in the name of Dominic Harris," CINDY says. "Anything else I can do for you?"

"Turn the lasers around this building off for about fifteen seconds?" I ask, voice full of sarcasm. There's no way she can...

"The grid within twenty feet of the exterior of this building will turn off for fifteen seconds, starting the second you close the exterior door." The interior door leading back to the brick closet slides open with a whoosh. "A car is waiting for you on the street directly west of this building. Good luck and good hunting."

This just in: Semi-sentient computers are creepy.

Chapter Fourteen

I have one of those confused waking moments when Sani gently shakes my arm in the morning. The pillows beneath my head are softer than anything I've ever touched. I'm cocooned in lavender-scented sheets of the highest thread count. The mattress is the most comfortable thing that's ever had the pleasure of supporting my weight. This is definitely not DIC.

Then I see the room's décor—colors that are meant to offend no one's taste, but don't really appeal to anyone's taste either—and remember I'm in a hotel.

Sani pulls open the curtains in my room, and I yank the covers over my head to defend my pupils from the onslaught of sunshine. I feel the light pressure of Sani sitting down on the bed next to me. The fact that Sani and I are both technically in the same bed stalls my brain's waking up. Through twelve years of the most rigorous training, my lungs have worked perfectly, but now they don't seem to be able to pull in enough air for the demanding activity of lying in bed.

Despite my best efforts, the covers inch away from my face, and I slam my eyes shut, groaning.

"Good morning, sunshine." His voice is as soft as the sheets wrapped around me.

I force one eye open, and he smiles at me. Oh, that smile. The one that makes my hearts want to jump out of my chest and join Sani's in his chest. That smile deserves two eyes gazing at it, so I open my other eye.

He laughs at me. "You're the grumpiest not-morning person I know."

Flinging my arms about, I toss myself dramatically onto my stomach and glance up at him. "Morning is a terrible time for operations. Ask anyone."

"But a good time for transnational flights to start." He's already fully dressed and ready to travel.

"Ugh." It's a reluctant agreement. "What time is it?"

"Eight. Dominic's flight leaves in two hours."

The silence between us while Sani waits for my brain to ramp up to operating speed is as comfortable as this bed.

Now that I'm fully conscious, yesterday comes rushing back to me. The image of Sani crumpled on the pavement, bleeding, flashes through my mind's eye. What a terrible day that went on forever—and it wasn't even a Monday. "How's your heart?"

His smile widens to a full-on grin. There's true happiness in it, the kind my soul can't help but swim toward, soaking in the light. "I'm good to go."

"As in…?"

"Yes." The relief in his posture matches my own. What we're going to attempt is crazy enough without Sani's dragon out of the game.

A grin invades my lips as if it's contagious. "Awesome." A growl comes from within me, but it's my stomach, not my dragon. "We have plans for breakfast?"

He points toward the door of my room that leads to the common area of the suite. "I ordered room service for you. Scrambled eggs with cream cheese, an entire plate of bacon, and pancakes with peanut butter and syrup."

The empty spaces inside my chest fill up until it feels like my rib cage won't be able to keep it all in. This is my absolute favorite breakfast, my big-day breakfast. I look at him and my lips fumble for words. I'm stuck in this half-space of wanting to both run away crying and tackle-hug him.

He reaches out to me and brushes a strand of hair back off my forehead and behind my ear. I'm so glad I'm lying down, because I don't think my knees have the strength to hold me up right now. "You don't have to say anything; the look on your face tells me I did well."

I find a word, the only word I need. "Perfect." Is this finally it? Is Sani finally seeing me like I see him? All it took was our entire race to be imprisoned and impending war with the mob to bring it out of him. I should feel guilty, but I can't find that emotion anywhere inside me.

I'm smiling up at him, trying not to look like the big honky doofus I feel like when a strange look flashes across his face. He pulls his hand stiffly back to his side and stands up. Everything inside me crumbles into a confused mass of hungry and tired.

"You should eat and get dressed." His words are cold and forced. "We need to leave soon."

"Yeah," is all I can manage. What the hell? Bipolar much?

I'm still trying to figure out what I did to make him do a total 180 when he shuts the door behind him on his way out of my room.

. . .

The cab is stuck in the perpetual traffic just outside of the airport. Sani and I haven't said a word to each other since he left my room. Dominic, of course, fills the silence with questions and comments and strategies and ideas. He rambles on like he's trying to make up time for all the watchful silence required of his job.

"I can try to get into the warehouse first and open a cargo door, so you can enter in dragon form," he says to me.

"If anyone's going to be able to get into the warehouse undetected long enough to open a cargo door, it's Sani," I respond. It's a mechanical statement, a fact. I keep all admiration out of my assessment. Well, at least I keep it out of my voice.

"Right," Dominic says. "We should do that instead, then."

Sani says nothing.

Thankfully, the cab pulls up to the correct gate entrance before Dominic can say anything else.

"See you on the west coast." Dominic climbs out of the cab and stretches.

"We'll be beside you the whole time," I remind him, warning him with my eyes.

The cab driver gives me an odd look in the rearview mirror, so I add, "You know, in spirit. So you don't have to worry."

"Sure," Dominic says, meeting my gaze for a long beat.

He doesn't have any luggage to speak of—I wouldn't let him go back to pack a bag—so he just waves and walks in through the sliding glass door. I watch him disappear in the mass of humanity, praying I'll see him again.

"You sure there's not somewhere else I can take you?" the cab driver asks us. The whole car smells like corn chips and baby powder.

"Nope," I answer. "The closest gas station is just fine." Sani and I had decided against asking him to drop us off in the closest remote area, figuring that would draw a little more suspicion than we need. People are kind of touchy about airports that way. I just need somewhere I can change out of sight, and we'll be on our way.

The cab merges into the traffic trying to escape the airport at ten miles an hour. I sigh and shift in my seat. Sani remains the kind of still that can drive a girl insane. I check out the traffic like it's the most fascinating thing on the planet. At this rate, Dominic will be in California before we make it off airport property.

I'm not a fan of texting and driving, but this cabbie is masterful. He picks up his phone at red lights and when traffic stalls, his fingers sliding across the screen even as he keeps up the cab-mandatory script: chit chat about our destinations, the weather, the local sports teams. Oh, and he's not wearing a seatbelt. I'm so glad my life (or at least my bodily health) is in this man's hands.

The traffic has cleared as we head out of the city. I pretend to stare out the window, but my full attention is focused on Sani sitting beside me as he starts to fidget. Every twitch of his fingers, every blink of his eye, sends a jolt of anxiety through my entire body. I can't figure out what's worse: the interminable stillness or the uncharacteristic fidgeting. What the hell is wrong with me? I'm about to make war against vicious killers, and all I can think about is why Sani went from hot to cold in two seconds this morning. He was so...*there*, and then he wasn't. What did I do?

This is why, even though I'm staring straight at it, I almost miss the gas station that passes by on our right. The one percent of my brain that's not currently obsessing over Sani reminds me of the mission.

"That was a gas station," I point out, my voice raising in pitch as it passes.

Sani startles and looks to where I'm pointing. Only then do I realize how odd it is that Sani didn't notice before me. Is it possible that something is distracting him as much as he is distracting me? And how high could our chances of success on this mission possibly be with both of us so preoccupied? If we stay like this, we'll be relying on Dominic to pull it off. My shoulders shudder as I picture that in my head. If we can't get our heads back in the game, Jacob is doomed.

"That gas station is no good," the cabbie says, dismissing it with a wave of his hand.

"Any gas station will do, really," Sani says.

"It's not a safe one for two young people." He eyes me in the rearview mirror. With my size and innocent face, I get this kind of thing a lot. People assume I can't take care of myself. It doesn't bother me, though; I use that to my advantage more often than not. I also figure the cabbie is doing his best to run up our fare. Since Wallace is paying for this, too, I don't mind so much. Dominic's plane doesn't take off for at least an hour, and I could probably use another ten minutes to refocus.

"Okay," I say. "But next one for sure. I don't care if it's in the middle of a war zone, got me?"

The man nods once and takes a left onto a less crowded street. I'm really watching the buildings we pass now, determined not to let this cabbie slip another one past us. We seem to have turned into a residential area. Not one of the good ones with white fences, perfect green lawns, and happy children, but the kind with barred windows, crumbling plaster, and cars on blocks. His driving deteriorates, taking corners too quickly and breaking the speed limit like whoa. What kind of game is this driver playing with us? Maybe he's planning to rob us and leave us in the ghetto. He'll have one hell of a surprise if he thinks we're easy marks.

Sani and I trade suspicious glances right before the cabbie makes a sudden turn onto a street just wide enough for one car. It's not really a street so much as a broken-down alley. There are other cars parked in the recesses between buildings surrounded by piles of trash and a problematic number of beer cans.

The sound of five hearts pounding inside the sudden quiet of the cab is deafening. Sani and I tense, each of us with a hand on a door handle. I expect the cabbie to turn on us with a gun pointing clumsily between the two of us, demanding our money and telling us to get out of the car.

That does not happen.

The passenger door on the junk-car closest to us swings open with surprising smoothness. It's an ambush.

"Get down!" I hiss at Sani. "Out of sight."

"You too," he says.

"No," I whisper as quietly as I can, hoping the cabbie won't hear me. "Whoever set up this trap knows me. I'm the only recognizable one. Stay down, we may get lucky."

Almost in sync with the other car, the cabbie opens his door and dives out into the alleyway. He didn't even bother to put the car in park. He scampers behind the car and ducks out of view. Now I think I know what all that texting was about. How stupid were we to assume a cab driver wouldn't recognize us from the news? Cabbies are the second-biggest gossips, next to hairdressers, of course.

Too late to do anything about it, I smell the telltale scents of CIA operatives: gunmetal, cheap suits, and too much aftershave.

At least fourteen armed men emerge from car doors and dark corners, but I only really see one. The sight of him brings my blood to a boil. My dragon cries out for retribution. An echoing cry escapes my lips. Before Sani can make a move to stop me, I'm standing in front of the cab, staring face to face with CIA agent Cleft Chin. He's never seen me in person before, but I'm confident he knows exactly who I am.

"Didn't expect to see you," I say. "Again."

He doesn't react to my implication. "Didn't expect to see you at all. Who knew Chen Lung's daughter would be stupid enough to take a cab when her face is plastered over every newspaper and TV screen?"

I shrug. "I'm told I'm full of surprises." I'm surprised at how nonchalant I sound, with my dragon roaring so loudly I can barely hear myself think.

"How about you surprise everyone by going completely against your race's nature and your personality profile and come with me to the D.I.C. quietly?"

I tap my chin like I'm thinking about it. I'm totally not. "What else does my personality profile say?" I ask—and not only because I just heard Sani sneak out of the cab door I left open and I want to keep Cleft Chin talking, but because I'm actually kinda interested. What do the shrinks think I'm capable of? Do they have any idea? I start to pace, swinging my arms, ensuring all eyes stay glued on me. Having no way of knowing where Sani went or what his plan is, I have to be ready for anything and make sure everyone is looking at *me*.

"Come in with me," Cleft Chin says. "I'll let you read it."

He sounds like a creeper, tempting a child with candy or a puppy. One thing is for sure: he has no respect for dragons. Maybe it's time I teach him some. I stop my pacing suddenly and turn to him, raising an eyebrow. His hand moves jerkily just a little toward his waist. I've been surrounded and feeling trapped, so only now do I realize how frightened this man is, despite his bravado. Taking a closer look at the improvised dragon trap they've turned this alley into, I realize a few things. There are only fourteen men here; no government vehicles, no air support, no snipers. That's about a fourth of what they had at the tea shop last night. Some of the men obviously aren't even CIA trained. Maybe local or state cops out of uniform. This was a rush job and Cleft Chin knows he's outgunned, but he's trying anyway. I'll say one thing for the guy: he's got balls. No brains, probably, but definitely balls.

"What if I were to make a trade?" I ask, letting my shoulders drop. It takes effort—staring at the man who handcuffed my wheelchair-bound father like I don't want to rip him into tiny little shreds—but I make my body language broadcast calm. I ball every bit of aggression into a tiny pit in my stomach and wrap it in layers of feigned cooperation. Whatever Sani's working on, I need to buy him as much time as possible.

"What kind of trade?" Cleft Chin asks. Relaxing, his hand moves to hang by his side once more.

"I'll come in with you. No trouble, I promise." I make a cross over my heart. "If you release my father."

Cleft Chin lets a loud, boisterous laugh escape. "That's impossible. Every single dragon threat must be eliminated."

Eliminated? That's a drastic word choice. Why not contained, or even neutralized?

As he says this, I spot a flicker of movement on the very edge of my vision. I don't draw attention to it, but I shake my head in apparent disapproval so I can survey the whole alley again. Hmm. There are only ten men still in sight. At first, the word "trap" comes to mind, but then I spot a still, shiny black shoe sticking out from one of the building corners. It is an ambush, after all. Of one. And I'm not the target.

"Why is it so impossible?" I ask quickly, before he notices my pause. "You get to take in one young and strong, impulsive and unpredictable dragon, and all you have to do is release a crippled old man."

"That crippled old man is more dangerous than ten healthy dragons put together," he says. Maybe he's not such an idiot, after all. He draws his eyebrows together and studies me. "But you know that, don't you?"

I do a quick survey of the alley around us. Only seven CIA men (or CIA posers) standing now. Plus the cabbie huddling behind the closest jalopy, but I really don't see him as a threat. I take him out of my mental calculations. Cleft Chin is going to notice his missing men any moment now; not even my scintillating conversation can distract him from the reduction of his team by half. It's time to move.

"Yeah." I start to shrug but turn the movement into a forward dive. As soon as my hands hit the grimy asphalt, I spring into a flip. I land three feet in front of Cleft Chin. His hand has reached the gun at his waist. Before he can grasp the grip, I kick his forearm away from his body and hear a light snap. Oops. Not really my fault. Human bone just breaks so easily, and I train with dragons. His gun clatters to the ground.

Before he's even finished crying out in pain, I spin behind him. Grabbing both of his arms, I pull them back. He groans in pain, but I ignore it. I position him between me and all of his men, who have their guns pointing in our direction. They're still underestimating dragon speed and strength, but a few more encounters like this and I won't be so lucky.

The sounds of multiple human hearts pounding seems to echo off the stained concrete walls of the alley. The smell of their sweat and their fear calls to my dragon, stirring it into a frenzy.

Somewhere to my left, Sani is grappling with one or more men. And, judging from the curses coming from that area, he's not having much trouble with them. Definitely local cops.

"Tell them to drop their weapons," I growl in his ear.

He speaks through clenched teeth. "Not a chance."

"You do realize the hard way is really only hard for you, right?" I tug on his arms to punctuate my point.

"I will never surrender to a *lizard*." The word is spat, like a curse, like a slur. So much hate packed into two tiny syllables.

This second, I know why he was chosen for this mission. And it's not because he's able to look my father in the eye without flinching. He said the dragon threat must be eliminated—not controlled or contained. Eliminated. I've seen this kind of hate before. With religious zeal, he believes dragons are dangerous. And evil. He doesn't just want to contain us, he wants to eradicate us. He's the most dangerous operative of all: a true believer.

My inner dragon smiles a toothy smile at the thought that enters my head. I'll show him something worth believing in.

"You don't like dragons too much, do you?" I ask.

"Like? Why would I *like* violent creatures who only live to serve themselves?"

"Oh, I have a German slash Japanese friend I'd love to introduce you to," I mumble.

"Huh?"

"Never mind. So." I let my smile enter my voice. "How do you feel about flying?"

"Sani!" I call, then glance around. I only see two other men standing in the alley. He's been busy.

"Yes?" he calls from my right. How the hell did he get over there? Gods, I love working with African dragons.

"Launch in five."

He doesn't have to confirm, I know he's ready.

I swoop down, scoop up Cleft Chin's gun, and make it intimately familiar with the back of its owner's head. The man goes limp and I support him with one of my arms under each of his underarms.

In human form, Sani sprints to the cab and grabs both of our packs.

"Three," I say.

"Two," Sani echoes, sprinting toward me.

On one, I shift violently into dragon shape. The two men

in the alley stumble back and raise their guns at me. What had been slender human arms are now two claw-tipped legs, looped underneath the agent's arms.

I shoot into the air and Sani leaps onto my back, as graceful as a panther climbing a tree. Cleft Chin dangles from my front claws, unconscious and unaware. A few shots whiz by us before I go invisible. Both men lower their guns, confusion painting their faces. The only thing they have to aim at now is their boss.

Now that I'm in the air, I can see the unconscious bodies littering the alley. While I was running my mouth, Sani took care of everyone else. My hearts lurch painfully, as if they're trying to ditch me and claim a spot next to Sani, where they really belong.

· · ·

"Why did you bring him?" Sani asks once we're high in the clouds.

I don't know. I hadn't really thought past him waking up miles above the city and hopefully crapping his pants. That was going to happen pretty soon. Then what?

I think my silence disturbs Sani, because he says, "You can't kill him."

"I hadn't been considering that," I say. "But remind me why not, again?"

"We're the good guys," Sani says.

"They don't think so." I motion to the city below us with my tail; by "they," I mean the general public, the CIA, the world. A world we've saved countless times, but that hates us because we're different from them.

"Since when have you let what someone thought about you define you?" His voice is soft and low, rumbling on my back.

Good point. Maybe since I realized what someone thought about me could also confine me.

The wind whips around my ears, producing a howling sound. I feel Cleft Chin's muscles tense under my claws as he wakes up. It takes a few seconds before he realizes where he is.

"Ahhh!" he yells. He looks up and behind him and, seeing nothing, screams again.

He stops screaming only when he runs out of breath.

"Wakey, wakey," I say.

"Put me down, right now!" he orders. As if he's in any position to be ordering me around.

"Oh! Sure! If that's what you really want." I loosen my grip a little and pitch forward.

The screaming sounds again, but I hear Sani's admonishing voice behind me. "Kitty."

"I was just having fun," I say, working a pout into my voice and playing up the bad cop persona. I straighten my flight path. "You never let me have any fun."

Cleft Chin's breaths are coming hard and fast now. Unfortunately, he hasn't soiled himself. We don't have much time before Dominic's plane takes off, so I'm going to have to make this faster than I'd like.

"Do you know what would happen if I dropped you right now?" I ask.

"Please don't." The man trembles in my grasp. His fear is a sharp taste on my dragon tongue, and it stirs my blood.

I let out an exaggerated sigh. "The CIA's never been

very good at answering questions."

"How did you know I'm CIA?" He seems offended, but doesn't deny it.

"You stink of it," I say. "Anyway. You would die. I could just let go and it would be as simple as that. If I wait a few more miles, nobody would probably ever find your body. Except maybe some wolves."

"What do you want to know?" Cleft Chin says quickly. "I have information. About your family, about the CIA's plans."

He gave in pretty quickly, letting me know I have to be more careful with this one: he's got nearly nothing to lose. "Oh, you seem to have misinterpreted my intent. That's really nice to know, though. My point is—killing you now would be so easy and would solve so many of my problems." I let that hover in the air around us and sink all the way in.

"But," Sani prompts, playing the good cop.

A hard wind blows and flutters Cleft Chin's jacket and pants. He sways a little, hanging from my claws, then groans. That couldn't have been timed better if I had planned it.

"But, I won't." I say.

"Not that I'm not grateful," Cleft Chin sputters, "but why not?"

I don't say: Sani won't let me. "Because I value human life. I've fought my entire life to protect the American ideals of life, liberty, and the pursuit of happiness. You're depriving my friends and family of two of those, but I still refuse to deprive you of the first. Do you want to know why?"

"Uh, sure?" I can tell he doesn't. All he's thinking about right now is how the baseball field below us is the size of a pinhead and what that means.

"Because you're the monster, not me." I say. "I may have

scales and claws and the ability to tear you limb from limb without breaking a sweat, but a monster exists in the mind. A monster is a creature of hate, not form."

"Okay, okay. I got it. You're not going to kill me because you're a wonderful person." I can almost taste the sarcasm in his words. "So can you let me down now?"

"Of course," I say, smiling. "You don't have to be so sarcastic, you know. If you get to know me, I'm actually pretty awesome. I'll put you down. But first, this info."

He spat. "Don't they train you on interrogative techniques? Why would I tell you anything now that I know you're going to let me go?"

"I *am* going to let you go. Unharmed, even. But where?" I shrug a little, making his feet kick at the open air. "I haven't decided yet. I do know this lovely little island that makes Gilligan's Island look like a suburb…"

I would love to spend hours listening to this guy whimper, but we're running out of time. Thirty hours until Jacob's deadline, and we keep crashing into new obstacles at every turn. I turn west and scan the ground for a nice, secluded spot.

Chapter Fifteen

We catch up with Dominic's plane over Kentucky after dropping Cleft Chin off in a deep valley in the Blue Ridge Mountains. Sani insisted on splinting his broken arm before we left, making us even later. It will be a few days before he sees another human soul again, but his survival training will keep him comfy until then. I sure hope he likes rabbit. I'm wiped after carrying him all that distance, but I'd rather he not be able to give a full report to his supervisors just yet. The fact that Sani's with me is still mostly a secret.

I hope.

Five hours later, we land at LAX. I find a nearby shipping container storage lot and drop down between two containers. Sani hops to a crouch on my back and takes a look around for a few minutes.

"No cameras," he confirms, jumping to the ground.

I let go of my invisibility and snap back to human form. Exhaustion overwhelms my entire body and I sway dangerously.

"Whoa, there," Sani says. He swoops in close to me and wraps steadying arms around my waist. "I think you overexerted yourself."

I lean in to his chest and let him hold even more of my weight, but I say, "I'm fine."

Laughing softly, Sani says, "If I know anything about women, it's that when they say they're fine, they mean the exact opposite."

He wraps one arm tighter around my waist, then places his other hand on the back of my head, pressing it gently to his chest. I sigh, relaxing. Then I realize he's never held me like this. For once, it doesn't feel careful or guarded. I'm painfully aware of every square inch of contact between our bodies. Every breath I take presses our hearts closer together. Something like an electric field crackles between us, and it recharges me.

"You just fought off a CIA ambush then raced a jet across the country," Sani says. "You can admit you need a break. It's not a weakness."

"We don't have time for a break. Dominic shouldn't be left alone for very long."

He pulls away to examine my face, but still supports most of my weight. My body aches with the sudden absence of his warmth and strength. His concerned green eyes take in everything. He's decided I'm okay for now, but he continues to hold me close. His gaze settles on my lips for a few seconds, then slides up to meet mine. Oh Gods, how my hearts pound. The heat of a blush sneaks up my neck and makes itself at home on my cheeks, leaving a blazing trail in its wake. Sani can definitely hear my frenzied pulse. Hell, as loud as it is, my father can probably hear it from here.

His full brown lips form an amused smile. A light glimmers in his eyes, glowing from a depth Sani rarely lets anyone see.

Barging into my thoughts like a world-class party pooper, the memory of his hot-to-cold behavior this morning terrifies me. I smile back at him as sweetly as I can, hoping to avoid another emotional shutdown. And they say *I'm* hard to read.

His hand around my waist starts rubbing tiny circles on my lower back. Nothing—and I mean nothing—has ever felt as good as this gentle pressure. Tendrils of pure bliss trace across my skin with every touch of his fingers.

I want to grab him and pull him against me until our lips crash together, but I catch myself. I've waited three years for Sani and—for whatever reason—he responds to my affection like a frightened animal, so patience is a virtue here. A torturous, impossible virtue.

I slide my hands slowly up his perfectly formed chest, the stony strength there belying the tenderness in his eyes. My fingers trail over his shoulders, then down the side of his arms, slowly tracing the cut of his triceps.

Need and want tighten my chest, degrading my saint-like patience. Being this close without getting closer is agony bleeding across every nerve ending. I slide my hands back up, over his shoulders, around his neck.

His grip around my waist tightens and fingers dig into my skin, pulling me closer to him. Our stomachs press together until the front of my body, from my knees to my chest, is joined with his. I've never felt more complete, like there's always been a piece of me missing, and Sani's touch has returned it to me.

He bends his head toward me, his eyes never flickering away from mine. There is nothing in the world except his arms around my waist and the space between our lips. His breath brushes across my lips, and the shock of it forces my eyes shut.

"Sani," I sigh. I don't remember telling my lips to make a sound, but there it is.

He freezes. His motion toward me a few seconds ago was so subtle and slow, but the absence of it is a sledgehammer to my heart. Arms fall from my waist, and a few steps place a chasm between us. All of my strength turns traitor and retreats with him. Or maybe it was never mine to begin with. I slump against a container.

"I'm sorry." He stares at my feet.

"You're sorry?" I want to scream, but it comes out more as a squeak.

Sani doesn't look at me. "Yes. I shouldn't have done that."

I'm done trying to figure him out. I need answers. "No? Why not?"

He swallows hard, his Adam's apple moving with painful slowness. "I just got caught up in the moment; it won't happen again."

"You didn't answer my question." My body is shivering with the effort of maintaining control. My throat painfully threatens to collapse on itself. "Caught up in what, exactly?"

"We should get going." He's calm with practiced restraint. "Dominic will be waiting for us."

Humans think it's painful when their heart breaks—try having two of them. It's a perfect description: heart break. Everything inside me feels like it's shattering into a million pieces, like the pain's too much to be contained by a single piece.

He looks around and starts walking in what I can only assume is the airport's direction.

"No!" I finally work up the strength to yell at his back. "Tell me why!"

"I don't want to lead you on."

He doesn't even turn around to deliver his lie. I know it's a lie. Leading someone on implies you don't care for them. He couldn't look at me and touch me like he just did and not care for me. Weak from hunger and exhaustion and probably something else I don't want to admit, I slide down the container and sit on the dusty ground, dropping my hands to my knees.

"Why are you doing this to me?" My traitorous voice cracks with unshed tears.

He stops walking but doesn't turn around. He just stands there, his back to me, his shoulders rising jerkily with his breath. For some reason, I know this is the moment. The moment when I can get through to him, crack this shell he's been hiding under. I just have to find the right thing to say. Too bad I've never been that great with words. So I decide to go with the truth. The truest truth I know, the one I've never even admitted to myself.

"I love you."

His breath stops. I *hear* him swallow his emotion. He shakes his head a little. "I know," he whispers, then keeps walking.

All right, that does it. Yeah, I love him. But right now he's pissing me off. There is something he's not telling me, and partners do *not* keep secrets from each other. I pull myself to stand up straight. My body doesn't deal with sadness very well, but anger—I thrive on that. I kindle it until it's a raging fire. My heartbeat and breath build up speed, eager for action.

I launch myself at Sani's back, zero to ninety in one stride. He doesn't expect it, so he has just enough time to turn around before I crash into him with a tackle the NFL would pay me millions of dollars for.

Even now, as we roll across asphalt and broken rocks, he positions his body to protect me from the worst of our uncontrolled tumble, wrapping his arms around me and turning so he absorbs impacts meant for me. Finally, we roll to a stop, and I make sure I land on top of him, pinning him to the rough ground. He may be bigger and quicker than me, but I'm stronger by twice, and I have the element of surprise. I mean, how many girls full-on tackle a guy after he completely rejects her?

"Kitty!" he shouts in surprise. "What are you doing?"

"You first. I *know* you care about me. I know it." His lips part to protest but I stop him. "Don't try to deny it, Sani. I know you better than anyone in the world. You may fool them with your lies, but you can't fool me."

He shifts his shoulders in a half-shrug, but doesn't try to deny it again. His eyes dodge mine.

"So what are you doing?" I ask. "You've avoided this conversation for years. You have to know what you do to me. Why are you doing everything you can to tear me apart?"

He continues to avoid my gaze, only fueling my fury. My pulse screams in my ears.

"Look at me!" I say.

He searches my eyes for so long, I don't think he's going

to answer. I've almost even forgotten what I asked and this me-straddling-him thing is beginning to get awkward. There's a war going on in his mind, and I see one side is starting to win. I hope it's my side, whatever that happens to be.

Finally, he licks his lips—let's skip right over what that does to the butterflies in my stomach—and speaks. "I'm trying to keep *us* from being torn apart."

I narrow my eyes at him. "You make absolutely no sense."

"Let me up and I'll explain."

I must look skeptical because he adds, "I won't walk away from you again."

"Promise?"

"With all my hearts," he says. The look he gives me then melts my soul into a little puddle. "I'm past the point of no return, anyway."

I crawl off him and leap to my feet. Sani stands stiffly, pain obvious in his movements.

"I'm sorry I tackled you," I say.

"I've had worse." He smirks and brushes dirt off his pants and shirt. "Plus, I deserved it."

I giggle. There's an ease to our conversation, like a weight's been lifted even though nothing has technically changed yet. "You did."

"We should walk while I explain."

I raise an eyebrow at him, crossing my arms stubbornly across my chest. I will not let him dodge this conversation again.

"I'm not avoiding again, I promise. We do need to get to Dominic soon, though. In case there's a kitsune around." He reaches out and takes my hand in his own, weaving our fingers together, and gently tugs me in the direction of the airport. "Please."

I walk next to him. To my surprise, he doesn't let go of my hand after I've given in. Also, to my annoyance, he doesn't say anything for a long while.

"So, about keeping us from being torn apart..." I prompt.

"I started falling for you the day we met." He stares straight ahead. There's not a shred of doubt in the statement. It's a fact he's sharing with me.

A gasp escapes my lips and I nearly trip over my own feet. Sani steadies me and patiently waits for it to sink in. "You never..."

"I know," he says. "I'm cautious, I guess. Everyone I've ever loved has been ripped away from me. I wanted to make sure it was real before I put myself out there."

He pauses for several seconds. I wait. What else can I do?

He runs a hand slowly over his hair, matching the motion with a deep breath. "A year after our assignment started, I decided it was time to make a move. So I asked your mother's permission."

My jaw drops as I look at him. "You asked my mother?"

"Old-fashioned?" he asks, a smirk playing at the corners of his full lips.

I laugh. "Totally."

"Not where I come from." He gets the sad faraway look that accompanies any mention of Uganda.

I squeeze his hand, bringing him back to the present. "So what'd she say?"

He shakes his head. "I get why," he says. "I know where she was coming from, especially considering the situation with your father."

"Sani." There's a threat in my tone. "What did she say?"

"She said I would get over it." This isn't even the beginning of the story, I can tell. My mother would never leave it at just that.

"And?"

He sighs, resigning himself to telling me the whole story. "And, in the meantime, I was not to engage in any romantic activity with you." His voice is stiff and detached, and I can hear my mother in his words.

"Why didn't you just say 'screw you' and do it anyway? I would have."

He smiles, knowing it's the truth. "She said if I did, she would have me transferred to the D.I.C. satellite office in Russia. I would never see you again."

"She was kidding," I say. "Wasn't she?"

He shakes his head and glances sideways at me, hesitant. Whatever he sees in my expression gives him the courage to continue. "A year ago, I went to her again. I told her that I'd really like her approval, but I didn't need it because I knew you had feelings for me, too. We work together every day, and it was killing me, piece by piece. Every time our hands brushed, I wanted to hold your hand. Every time a guy at school checked you out, I wanted to shove him in a locker. I could barely stand it every time you looked at me, begging me to make a move, knowing I couldn't do it."

My breath catches in my throat at his confessions. Every word sends my hearts crashing wildly against my ribcage. I swallow against the lump in my throat, but it comes right back.

"All this time…" I start to say.

Sani stops walking and turns to stand in front of me, taking my other hand in his. Several seconds pass before his eyes stop searching for somewhere else to look, and his gaze settles uncertainly on mine. "I told her that I loved you, and I *wasn't* going to get over it."

Wait, had I passed out when we landed and now was hallucinating? Or did Sani really just say that he loved me? I squeeze his hands. They feel real enough. Though to be honest, I don't know what hallucinated hands would feel like.

"Kitty?" His voice is as soft and sweet as cotton candy. The uncertainty on his face convinces me this is really happening. "You still with me?"

"Yeah, um." I look into his cool green eyes to steady myself. We've wasted so much time. It's like we were playing chicken and we both swerved when we should've crashed into each other. How much energy had we wasted, trying to keep our true feelings buried under others when we were both dragons? "What did she say to that?"

He shrugged. "She didn't say anything, just dismissed me. But the next day, I saw Director Bean in the hall and he said that he was really going to miss me, especially how polite and not troublesome I was—I think that was a dig at you—when I left in three days for Russia."

"She transferred you? But you didn't go anywhere." Rage, familiar and hot, slides through my veins. My own mother. How dare she!

"I went back to her on my hands and knees and begged her to undo it," he says. He looks away for a second and coughs gently. I know that look well; if he were human, his eyes would be sparkling with tears.

"How'd you convince her?" I ask. "When she's made her mind up about something, there's no going back."

"I gave my word I'd keep my hands off of you and promised to continue to keep you out of trouble. I said if she knew any other operative who could — " He has the decency to look apologetic here " — temper your, uh…impulsiveness as well as I could, I'd gladly take the job in Russia. She saw my reasoning and trusted me to keep my promise. I think she knew you were better off with me as your partner."

Mouth slightly parted, I stare at him for a few seconds. This is all too much. My mind races with a thousand different thoughts. Then I stomp forward at a quick jog.

Sani quickly catches up with me. "Where are you going?"

"First I'm going to rescue Jacob. Then I'm going to rescue my mother," I say. "So I can kill her."

Sani stops. "Kitty, wait." He grabs my arm and spins me around. "Please."

It's the pleading that makes me stop and stare up into his beautiful, hopeful eyes.

"What?"

His voice is so fragile, like he's simultaneously afraid and hoping I'll break him. "Can I kiss you now?"

A grin explodes onto my face. I jump up, wrapping my arms around his neck and my legs around his waist. Yeah, a little hasty, but we've both been waiting for this moment for three excruciating years. I think we've moved slowly enough. He answers my grin with one just as wide.

"I want to try this again, in case you didn't catch it the first time," he says and pauses to stare deep into my eyes, placing a hand on either side of my face. "I love you. I have for years."

My hearts burst into fireworks; I don't know any other way to describe this feeling. "I love you!"

He leans his head forward and I meet him halfway, our lips touching tentatively at first. Then he presses his full lips against mine and opens his mouth just a little, like a question waiting for an answer.

Oh man, do I have an answer for him.

I'm filled with this desperate feeling, like I can't get close enough to him. I press my lips harder against his. Every touch, every movement sends a thrill through my stomach.

His arms circle my waist, gentle at first, but then he presses his hands against my back and pulls me against him, deepening our kiss. My head spins in the most delicious way. There's nothing in the world except for me, Sani, and the scant space between our bodies. The way his lips move against mine is like a promise, an apology, and a declaration all rolled into one.

I have no idea how long it is before Sani reluctantly pulls his lips away. Like the separation pains him and he has to make up for it somehow, he rests his forehead against mine.

"If we don't stop now, I never will," he says.

I'm having serious trouble getting enough oxygen. "I know the feeling."

He gently lowers my feet to the ground and places a kiss on my temple, sending warm shivers through my entire body.

"Right," I say. "Rescues first, making out later. You never let me have any fun."

. . .

Dominic is sitting on a planter in the passenger pickup area of LAX. "What happened to you two?"

I look down and see the brand new gaudy Washington D.C. tourist clothes I bought at the hotel this morning are dirt-stained and torn here and there. Sani looks worse.

I shrug. "Ran into a little trouble, nothing we couldn't handle." No need to tell him the CIA's on my back, right? Or that I tackled Sani in a storage yard because he wouldn't kiss me. He'd have a field day with that little tidbit.

Dominic's eyes travel down to our joined hands, and he smirks. "I *knew* you two had something going on."

Well, this is super awkward. None of us say anything for a good forty-five seconds but, to Sani's credit, he doesn't let go of my hand.

"What's the plan?" Dominic finally asks.

Oh, right. The plan. I should probably get one of those.

"First, Kitty needs to rest," Sani says.

Dominic and I both begin arguing with him at the same time.

"I don't care," Sani says, holding up his hands as if to stop the words we fling at him. "She almost passed out when we landed and, we all know, no matter what our plan is, she's going to be doing the heavy lifting tonight. A high-calorie meal and some time sitting down, at the very least."

Something troubling churns to the surface of my thoughts. "Tonight?" I ask.

"Yeah, that's when we're going to make our move, right?" Dominic says.

"The president said we only had forty-eight hours," Sani reminds me. "Which gives us until mid-afternoon tomorrow, at the latest."

Dominic walks to the curb to hail a cab. I have ghetto-alley flashbacks and my entire body tenses with reluctance. "Maybe we should walk?"

"Walk?" Dominic says. "This is L.A., kiddo. And I thought you needed to rest?"

Sani looks between us, me biting my lip in anxiety, Dominic looking at me like I'm ridiculous. "Give her your hat."

Dominic does as he's told. I hold it between my thumb and index finger, like it might bite me. Or make my hair smell bad, at the very least.

Sani turns and walks about thirty feet to a slightly overweight middle-aged woman looking up and down the street for her ride. He pulls out his wallet. "How much did those sunglasses cost you?" The aforementioned sunglasses are sitting on her head, nestled in a mess of dyed blond curls and currently unused.

She takes her time letting her eyes travel up and down his lithe form. Does she have no shame? Sani's nearly young enough to be her son. Granted, he is the one person in the world who can look like he's ready for a *GQ* shoot after traveling across the country in convenience-store sweats.

"Just seven dollars, honey," she drawls. "You like them?"

She definitely straightens her back to push her considerable boobs further into his view. Self-conscious, I frown at my own non-existent chest.

Gods bless him, he doesn't even notice, but he sweetly smiles down at her. "My girlfriend is having a terrible migraine right now and she forgot hers. I'll give you twenty dollars for them."

The woman's boobs deflate at the word "girlfriend," but I have quite the opposite reaction. Girlfriend. I'm his girlfriend. Wait, or was that just another part of his lie? Being a spy is so complicated sometimes.

She slides the glasses off her head and hands them to him, snatching the twenty dollar bill from Sani's hand. "You have a deal, sugar pie."

Sugar pie? Where the hell is this woman from?

He walks back over to us and wipes the sunglasses thoroughly on his shirt before sliding them gently onto my face. The soft brush of his fingers against my temples sends a thrill through my arms, down to my fingertips. "Make sure your purple stripe is completely hidden inside the hat. There is a much bigger Chinese population here than in D.C., so hopefully that will play to our advantage."

"Why don't you just dye your hair back to its natural color?" Dominic asks. "The purple kind of stands out."

"This *is* my natural color," I say.

He points at the strand that's only halfway tucked into the hat. "*That* is not natural."

"All Chinese dragons have a stripe of brightly colored hair," I explain. "My mother's is red, my father's is blue. Mine is purple."

"And dye won't hold in our hair," Sani adds. "Just like tattoo ink won't stay in our skin."

"Weird," Dominic says, shrugging.

All three of us walk to the curb as Dominic puts up his hand again. My hearts pound in anticipation of being trapped in another one of those traitor-machines. My dragon begs to let her fly instead, but I know Sani's right about at least one thing: I need some rest. My legs feel like they're about to collapse underneath me.

"Where are we going?" Sani asks.

"You need lots of food, right?" Dominic grins like a maniac. "In-N-Out!"

"That sounds dirty," I say.

"Yeah," Dominic agrees. "You're going to love it."

"About tonight," I say as cabs pass by Dominic without

slowing.

"What about it?" Dominic asks.

"I'm not sure it's the right time. The Yakuza are a massive crime organization, essentially," I say.

Sani catches on to my meaning right away. "And violent crime is mostly done at night."

"Yeah, so maybe nighttime isn't the best time to hit them," I say. "What if they're coming back from a drug deal— or worse, a gun deal—when we roll in? They'd be fully armed and hopped up on adrenaline."

"Director Bean is working with them," Sani added. "He trained us. He'd expect us to attack at night."

"Not to mention humans always let their guard down when the sun's up," I add. "They feel safer."

"So when were you thinking?" Dominic asks.

It physically pains me to say this. "Early morning."

Sani lets out a harsh sigh. "That doesn't leave us much time to regroup if it turns out Jacob isn't there."

"It's the only place that makes sense," I say. "And we know Director Bean is there for sure."

"Let's face it," Dominic says, voicing the fear we're all afraid to talk about. "If Jacob's not there, we're screwed, no matter when we go."

He's right, of course. If Jacob's not at the headquarters, he's dead, and I lose any goodwill I have with the president and the American people. Without those things, any chance I have of seeing my family and dragon friends again plummets to immaterial levels. I have twenty-four hours to save my friend from mobsters or literally all hope is lost. And with that cheery thought, we all get in a cab.

Chapter Sixteen

It turns out In-N-Out is just a burger joint. The best burger joint in the entire world, but fast-food burgers all the same. I have to hand it to Dominic, he was right about one thing at least: I love this place. Sani sits next to me with a graveyard of burger wrappers in front of him and Dominic sits across from us, slack-jawed.

"For such a small girl, you sure eat a lot," he says. The harsh fluorescent lights cast shadows on Dominic's face, making him look as tired as I feel.

I'm washing my third 3 x 3 down with a chocolate shake when a nine-to-five white collar slumps into the booth next to us, his back facing me. We have to keep the spy and dragon talk down to a minimum with a human so close to us. The cabbie back east taught us that anybody could be a threat, even the most unassuming characters.

"Changing makes us very hungry," Sani says, as cryptically as he possibly can. "It burns a lot of calories, to say the least." He leans forward, placing his forearms on the fake granite table. The way his biceps bunch underneath the cotton fabric of his shirt has me completely distracted until Dominic speaks.

"I thought you were just typical teenagers."

No one has ever called me typical. I can't say I like it.

"I could hunt instead," I say, in between shoving fries in my mouth, the salty, starchy goodness muffling my words.

"Hunt?" Dominic's eyebrows twist in a combination of disgust and suspicion.

"Yeah, I hear there are a lot of cattle farms around here. That would be perfect." I'm just messing with him; greasy burgers and fries are so much more delicious than swallowing a cow whole. Trust me on that one. But you do what you have to while staking out political refugees in rural Argentina.

Once the guy at the next booth gets his burger unwrapped and firmly set in one hand, he picks up an iPad mini and starts awkwardly flicking through a news site with his thumb. I will him to click on one of the celebrity gossip stories—I haven't been able to get my fix in days—but my mind control powers are as nonexistent as they ever were. He taps an article and whose photo pops up in full color on the screen? Your friendly neighborhood Chinese dragon. I tug the baseball cap lower on my head and try to read over his shoulder, but can only catch words like "dangerous," "menacing," "threat," and "confined." I'm sure it's a cheery article, full of dragons dancing through sunshine and rainbows, helping old ladies cross the road, and rescuing puppies.

Sani notices where my attention's gone and his eyes snap to the same screen. I catch one more thing on the article before the man flicks back to the main news page: a picture. Liquid hydrogen floods my veins, and I just about choke on some fry crumbs.

A picture of Director Bean with the words "sought for questioning" attached. It's his official government headshot, the one hanging on the walls of DIC. His eyes stare out from the screen and pierce my lungs, leaving me short of breath.

Dominic finally notices us staring when we both let out a gasp. He starts to turn around but Sani stops him with a small shake of his head. Dominic presses his lips together and gives us a disapproving glare. He really doesn't like being out of the loop, not one bit, but at least he has the sense to heed my partner's warning.

My mouth goes dry. What kind of questioning, exactly, did they want Bean for? Was it the "polite chat in a wood-paneled office" kind of questioning or the "private plane ride to a facility that doesn't technically exist" kind of questioning? Sani slips his hand beneath the table and grabs mine. Warmth floods from my fingertips up through my arm to my entire body, smothering the rising panic. I pull in a slow breath and refocus on the mission. There's nothing we can do about Bean now. If he doesn't want to be found, I definitely don't want to go looking for him.

"So we're all agreed tomorrow morning is the best time?" I ask.

Dominic purses his lips and nods. Sani says, "Yes."

"We need to find somewhere to lay low for the night, then," I say.

My cell phone rings. I jump, then pull it out of my pocket and frown at the screen. Another different unknown number. I'm getting so tired of this crap. I don't even enjoy talking on the phone to people I like.

Sighing, I flip it open. "Hello?"

"Good afternoon, Kitty." CINDY's programmed cheer greets me. "I am just about to shut down for a few hours to run a diagnostic and wanted to make sure there wasn't something I could do for you before."

I do a quick scan of the immediate area, looking for cameras and microphones. I fail to find any, but I know well enough that doesn't mean anything. "Were you listening to us?"

"Would you like me to?" she asks. "Wallace doesn't have me listen in on the ones we know are friends."

"You are seriously creepy, CINDY."

"I apologize," she says. "I've been monitoring the news feeds and, since the president's son hasn't been returned, I assumed your mission was not yet complete."

I don't respond. What am I supposed to say to that? For a second, I had almost forgotten I wasn't talking to a real, live human.

"So you do not need anything?" She sounds almost sad.

"Actually," I say, smiling. "We could use another hotel."

"No problem." A pause. "I found an available suite within walking distance of your current location. I will text you the address."

I swallow hard. Knowing how accurately and quickly CINDY had tracked our location set my nerves to vibrating. "Thank you."

When this is all over, Wallace and I are going to have a serious chat.

• • •

After the longest, hottest shower I've had in years and changing into a fresh set of badly fitting clothes from the hotel lobby's gift shop, I meet Sani and Dominic in the living room of our suite at around two in the afternoon—five, D.C. time. This place is absolutely gorgeous with real wood furniture, carpets like clouds, and marble everything. I'm giving serious consideration to letting Wallace pay for all my accommodations in the future. If I pull off freeing the dragons, it will be the least he can do. Who knew the guy who wore ratty T-shirts with obscure computer references on them every day was this loaded? He could pay someone to dress him.

Sani's sitting on a plush taupe loveseat that sits parallel to a mahogany coffee table with intricate scrollwork all around it. Dominic is sitting in one of two matching chairs on each end of the table. I hesitate, eying both the empty chair and the spot beside Sani. Emotions are running so high today, and we've been dancing around each other for so long, I don't know where I stand. And I certainly don't know where to sit.

He pats the spot next to him and smiles. My hesitation disappears. It's like his smile is the sun, coming out from behind dark clouds and warming me to my toes. When I go to sit next to him, he puts his hands on my waist and pulls me into his lap. I lean against his firm chest and lay my head on his shoulder as arms of lean muscle wrap me in a cocoon.

Dominic raises an eyebrow at us. I don't want to think about it now, but Sani and I are going to have to be careful about our relationship if things return to normal.

Rather, *when* they return to normal. When, not if. This is what I keep trying to tell myself.

I yearn for normal, my kind of normal, anyway. But I don't want my mother sending Sani to Russia or Mongolia or wherever. Not now, when he's finally opened up to me.

The flat-screen TV on the wall is on CNN and just loud enough that I can hear the reporter's words. For once, we're not the story. They're showing a video of a cheerleader falling on her face at a pep rally. The same fifteen-second clip has been repeated at least five times. She's not injured, so I don't think it's actually news, but who am I to judge? American media confuses me more than advanced cryptography.

Sani's taken a shower too; the scent of lemongrass and mint flows from his skin with an undercurrent of something raw and robust that is just pure Bulisani Mathe. I inhale a deep breath, taking his scent into my lungs and holding it there.

"Just to clarify," Dominic says testily.

I exhale in a rush, scowling at him from the corner of my eye.

He continues with measured words. "We're about to break into a mafia stronghold to rescue a teenage boy who may or may not be there."

"And interrogate and either rescue or capture the current slash former head of DIC," I add with a "what's your point" undertone.

"Exactly," Dominic says. "So maybe you two should tone down the googly eyes for a few hours?"

I slice a glare at him, but slide to the seat next to Sani. "Okay, Mister Secret Service Man, what's the plan?"

We argue about our plan of attack for an hour, but we make progress and come up with something we can all live with. It's not a perfect plan—but they really never are, are they? Still, it feels like we're missing something on this one, like a black hole in the middle of it all that we can't even focus on properly.

We're just about to break for the night—well, half the night—when a familiar face staring back at me from the TV screen stops me cold. Even in a copy of an official agency photo reproduced on this flat-screen, it feels like Director Bean is staring straight at me, admonishing me for not following orders. His gray eyes drill into me, nailing me to my spot on the couch.

"Turn it up," I say to no one in particular. I have no idea where the remote is, but I can't tear my eyes from the screen to look for it.

Sani focuses on the screen and pops up from the loveseat to turn the volume up on the TV manually. Who knew you could do that?

He rejoins me as the reporter's high, clear voice fills the room. "It is unclear whether the former spy is in hiding of his own accord or if he has been detained by an unknown party. All we're being told is that he has worked extensively with the dragons in the past and is wanted for questioning by the newly formed Senate Committee dealing with dragon affairs."

Try to get the Senate to halt a war or fix the national debt, and they can't be bothered to show up—but there's already a committee to deal with the dragons. I suppose it doesn't matter that we've been doing fine without a committee to oversee us for several millennia. The woman speaking has perfectly styled shoulder-length blond hair and the kind of face you think is pretty when you're looking at it, but immediately forget about when you look away. She turns to face a different camera, and the screen seamlessly splits in two, with her face on the left side and what looks like a protest in front of the Capitol building on the other.

"In related news," the woman says, "The NAACP, PETA, Amnesty International, and other civil rights organizations are calling for the release of any dragons who are being held without formal charges."

"PETA?" I say, standing and moving closer to the screen. "Really?" They're doing more harm than good. We're not animals.

Another person appears on the right side of the screen, a man, a representative from Amnesty International according to the text on the bottom of the screen. "This is no different than any other concentration camp or racial segregation, another embarrassment to this country's history of tolerance and acceptance. I'm receiving reports from trustworthy sources that some of these dragon shapeshifters have served this country for years, fighting against terrorist threats. At the very least, they're victims of irrational prejudice. At most, they're heroes." His face is so sincere and sympathetic, a twinge smacks my hearts inside my chest.

The right side of the screen then shows a close-up of the protestors. There are only about thirty of them, but Gods bless them they're energetic. And they have catchy picket signs, like: "Set the dragon-people free!" and "Dragons are people, too!" and "End Racial Segregation! Again!" I'd laugh if the reason why those signs exist wasn't so sad.

"See," Sani whispers in my ear. I have no idea when he moved to stand behind me. "They don't *all* hate us."

The image on the right changes again to the security footage of Wallace's change, still the only image of a dragon form available. I know the truth: that he was just panicking, scared and inexperienced. But even I'll admit he looks dangerous and out of control, representing everything the CIA claims they're trying to protect the American people from. If I were a mom sitting at home with little children in my quiet suburb, I'm not sure how I'd feel about the scene. Would I be scared enough to support the incarceration of an entire species? Being honest with myself, I can't say I wouldn't. And that, more than anything, terrifies me. When you can empathize with your enemy, you're half lost.

The reporter continues to talk over the image, but I don't hear her anymore. I'm watching Wallace change over and over again, hearing Cleft Chin utter "lizard" on repeat in my head. I was wrong. We *are* the monsters, at least as far as most Americans are concerned. We're Frankenstein's monster, misunderstood with the villagers lighting their torches and waving their pitchforks. The images scream inside my brain, rising to a fever pitch.

Dominic is sneaking off to his bedroom for the night. All of a sudden, I realize what our plan is missing, the lost puzzle piece. The clamor in my mind falls away.

"We're changing the plan," I snap, stopping Dominic in his tracks. He turns slowly, half annoyed, but half curious, too.

"Kitty," Sani says gently. "We all agreed."

"Yeah, but we had faulty parameters," I say, returning to the loveseat. I sit cross-legged on the cushion with my elbows on my knees and fingers folded underneath my chin. "Sani and I are still thinking like it's three days ago, like we still need to keep dragons a secret. The whole world knows we exist now. The game has changed."

"I don't believe it's wise to throw away that caution; knowing and seeing are two different things," Sani says, moving to sit next to me. He's speaking from experience, I know, but this is too important to let fear of hurting his feelings get in the way.

"That's because not revealing our dragon forms has been drilled into your head by your DIC trainers," I say. There's a warning in my voice. I don't want to bring up his past, but I will if I have to.

Dominic stands back from us. He knows there's more to this than what we're both saying and, for once, is wise enough to butt out.

"You know what exposing yourself as a dragon could lead to," Sani says, his voice cracking. "It's too dangerous."

I reach out and put a steadying hand on his arm. "Sani, this isn't Uganda. We aren't your parents."

"I don't see any difference," he says.

I point at the television. "That's the difference! They already know exactly what we are. They're still trying to figure out what to think of us. Right now, the only image they have of us is a terrifying one that breeds hate and fear. They already know who and what I am. I want to give them another image."

A terrible silence falls over the room. My eyes plead with Sani to see past his fear and his experience to the new world we could make.

"You want people to see you rescuing Jacob," Dominic says from his dark corner. He understands, I can hear it in his voice.

"I want *everyone* to see me—a dragon—rescuing Jacob, taking on the deadliest criminal organization in the country to return their precious First Son safe and sound. I want to shove it in their faces until they can't deny what it means. I want the president to watch me, on TV, cleaning up a mess that humans created and couldn't fix themselves."

"You're a spy, not a PR person," Sani says. "It's not your job to change public opinion. Your job is kind of the opposite."

I know that he's only being so cautious because of what happened to his family, but he's starting to get on my nerves. He's so perceptive. Why can't he see what the rest of the world is seeing at this moment? We're so far out of the closet at this point nobody even remembers the closet exists, except for us.

"Who else is going to do it?" I ask him. "Like I said, the game has changed. We're stuck in the middle of a war that's being fought in the media. If you can think of any other way to counter the lies the CIA is spreading about us, I'll gladly do it your way."

"She's right, you know," Dominic says, looking at Sani. "I don't know what happened to your parents in Uganda, but I can guarantee the dragons have never seen a situation like this."

Sani shakes his head, but it morphs, and then he nods slowly. Look at Dominic being all reasonable and helpful. I'm so proud. My unlikely ally.

"If Kitty ever wants to go out in public again, or see her parents again, the American public has to rally behind her enough to convince the president to go against the CIA."

Okay, so maybe I underestimated the guy. A faraway smile spreads across his face. Or maybe not.

I look at him with one raised eyebrow, figuring out the

source of his enthusiasm. "And you'd be the guy who helped us do it."

He grins. "I'll definitely get a book deal. Maybe a TV show. The camera loves this face." He strolls back to his chair, pointing at his face.

I roll my eyes as hard as I can. "At least somebody does."

Why Dominic supports my plan is inconsequential, as long as he follows through.

I turn to my partner. "What do you say, Sani?"

He stares hard at my wide, hopeful eyes for several minutes. I can't begin to imagine the scenes playing in his head right now. The government he worked for in Uganda killed his parents in front of him because someone found out they were more than human. It was a classic witch-hunt scenario, a burning stake and everything. I take his hands into my own and squeeze, pressing our clasped hands against my chest in an attempt to bring him back from that dark place. I need him here, in this moment. We all do.

His eyes finally refocus on the present and his tortured gaze meets mine. "I suppose I should at least hear your plan before saying no."

Chapter Seventeen

I wake up for the fourth time since lying down. Why does my overactive mind refuse to let my exhausted body get some rest? I've tried reasoning with it, threatening it, even counting imaginary English dragons. Growling at the cool night air, I roll over to look at the clock: 1:20 in the morning. The green lines burn into my vision, searing the numbers on my brain, reminding me how tired I'm going to be in the morning. We're leaving in less than five hours, and I've probably only stolen about an hour of sleep so far.

The mattress is incredibly soft and fluffy, but now it just feels like it's sucking me in, partnering with the thick blanket to smother and incapacitate me. How can I be taking so many breaths and still be so short on air? I stare at the ceiling, trying to will myself back to sleep until it becomes obvious that's not going to happen anytime soon. I climb out of the suffocating covers and stare out the window at a city that has no idea what's coming for it tomorrow. More cars than I would have expected still race down the highways, nothing but blurs of red and white lights from my view far above the city streets. I think about the protesters on the TV earlier and wonder how many Americans side with them — and how many would side with Cleft Chin. How many people on the street far below me right now would turn me in? How many would shelter me? I'm not a betting girl, but I'd wager the former far outnumbers the latter.

I check my pack, still stuffed to the brim with guns and grenades I hope I don't get the chance to use. Despite our rather violent history, dragons aren't generally fond of using human weapons. It's completely unnatural and feels entirely *wrong*. It seems like something always goes wrong when gunpowder is involved. We're messing with something we have no business messing with. Sometimes, though, you have to do things you don't enjoy. In my line of work, those times come more often than not.

Speaking of things I enjoy, my brain reminds me of the chocolaty snacks I saw on the mini-bar earlier today. What a perfect distraction for my racing, self-doubting mind, not to mention perfect fuel for a body that's about to change more times in a day than it's used to in a week. Now that I'm out from under the thick covers, the cool air is a little too much for my bare arms and legs, so I grab the plush robe hanging in my room's closet and tie it loosely around my waist. The robe was made for a normal-sized adult, so it repeatedly catches between my feet and the floor, but the material is kitten soft and I melt into it.

The door opens silently with a gentle push from me, and I pad almost silently across the soft carpet to the kitchen area. A high-calorie, high-fat, high-sugar feast lies before me — just the thing for the night before a big mission. A king-sized package of Reese's peanut butter cups calls my name, and I tear it open. The rustling of the package is like a gunshot in the silence of the hotel room. As hard—and as slowly—as I try, I can't get the wrappers to quiet down. A flicker of movement out of the corner of my vision hijacks my attention, and I spin toward it, dropping my snack on the marble counter. My hearts jump-start and pound at full speed.

A figure stands on the balcony on the other side of the living room, shrouded in almost complete darkness. The lights from the city below are just enough for me to tell it's a man. Or maybe an incredibly tall, well-built, boob-less woman with no hair. I crouch low and watch it just over the top of the kitchen counter, but it doesn't move for several seconds. My lungs ache against my ribs, but I keep my breathing under control with shallow, quick breaths.

Crouched, I scoot to the end of the counter, readying myself to leap from my hiding place and surprise the intruder. I jump to my feet, but it doesn't go like it had in my head. The belt of the robe catches on a scrollwork drawer handle, throwing me off balance. Then I trip over the folds of cloth gathered around my feet.

I fall flat on my face. The super-soft cloth does very little to cushion my fall as various joints and pieces of flesh smack against the cold tile.

The gentle swoosh of French doors opening is followed immediately by a soft chuckle. Alarm and tension flee from my body, leaving only utter chagrin in their wake. The bruises the floor gave me are nothing compared to the bruises purpling up my pride.

"Kitty." Sani strides quickly to where I lay sprawled on

the icy kitchen floor. "What are you doing?"

I have never felt so embarrassed in my entire life. Not even when the prime minister's daughter caught me digging through a drawer of panties I thought had belonged to her mother—nor when I'd stuttered through that ridiculous story, trying to explain the situation. Some super-spy I am.

"I was just about to unleash hell on an intruder," I say, groaning and fumbling in the plush layers.

He places his arms under mine and pulls me up, examining me. "Yes, you're fierce as a lion on the Serengeti."

I blush and look at my feet. "Yeah, a cub before its eyes have even opened." I probably look like a little girl wearing her mom's bathrobe. All I need is some too-bright blush and uneven lipstick smeared across half my face. Sani, on the other hand, looks like a freaking fitness model in his red tank top and gray basketball shorts.

"Did you hurt anything?" he asks.

I shake my head. "Not really."

He scoops up my abandoned midnight snack and a Snickers bar before guiding me to the loveseat with a hand against my lower back. "Couldn't sleep?"

"My brain won't shut off." I sigh, surrendering to him.

He sits down cross-legged and pulls me into his lap, handing me my candy. "I know the feeling." He wraps the robe securely around me, smirking at his deliberate actions, before opening his own candy bar.

We munch on our chocolaty, sugary goodies in silence, staring into space. Thousands of things we should be saying vibrate in the air between us. I reach into the package for the last peanut butter cup only to find that I've already eaten it. Sani's wrapper is empty, too, so we just sit there, the distant noises of the city streets the only sound in the room. Neither of us looks at the other.

"Are we doing the right thing?" Sani finally says.

I want to just say "yes," confidently with no reservations. I want to tell him I know exactly what I'm doing, and everything's going to turn out peachy. But Sani's the only person I refuse to lie to. I crumple the candy wrappers in my fist and squeeze tight. The sharp corners of the cardboard stab at my palms, bringing my thoughts into focus.

"My mom once told me if you're asking yourself that question, you're at least on the right track."

He nods. "Your mom's a wise woman."

I look straight into his eyes then. They glint yellow sparks in the darkness. "She's not always right, though," I say.

With me sitting in his lap, our faces are level. All I have to do to kiss him is lean forward just a few inches. But I guess I'm still scared of frightening him, of pushing too far and making him push me away again. It's harder than I thought to forget years of what felt like rejection, even now that I know what it really was.

A grin slides across my face and Sani's eyebrow raises in response. "How are you feeling?" I ask.

"I told you. Good as new."

I waggle my eyebrows as I take the candy wrapper from him and toss both of them onto the coffee table. "Are you sure?"

"Yes." A smile cracks his serious expression. "What are you up to?"

"I'm just thinking maybe we should make sure you're completely better. You know, for the mission."

His teeth flash bright in the darkness. "You want to go

flying."

I leap to my feet and tug on his arms. "A little moonlight stroll."

He says, "That's entirely against protocol," but he follows me to the patio doors without any resistance.

The half moon is bright and clear, more than enough light for us to see everything in perfect detail.

Feeling giddy with Sani's touch and maybe a slight sugar rush, I climb up onto the patio railing, standing on four inches of burnished bronze. I face him. "Ready?" I do a back flip into the night air and let the dragon rush over me.

When I don't immediately go invisible, Sani glances nervously at the other balconies. "Someone might see you."

I don't care. Tomorrow I'm going to broadcast my true nature to the entire world. What does it matter if a few rich people get a sneak peek? Sani cares, though, and maybe he's partially right. We don't want the CIA showing up before we have a chance to follow through on our plan.

"You better get on quick, then," I tease.

"Kitty," he warns.

"Sani," I mock his tone. "Come on, let's see what two healthy hearts gets you."

He scans the hotel building, but even serious Sani can't stop the smile that inches onto his face. He's been too long out of dragon form.

The green-gold of his eyes latches onto me and I couldn't move if I wanted to. His pupils elongate as his dragon takes hold. A sleek, black shape crouches low on the patio. Fully grown African dragons aren't very much bigger than their human forms, but they are ten times as powerful and quick. Sani stretches the full length of his lithe midnight body. His downy earflaps slap against the soft fur of his face when he shakes his head. I'm overwhelmed with a sense of *rightness*, and I can't tell if it's coming from Sani or me.

Moving with the grace of a panther and the raw strength of an alligator, he soars over the patio railing and lands effortlessly on my back. "Let's go," he whispers.

I jet straight north. Only minutes pass before we enter the Angeles National Forest and I swoop low, gliding through valleys and flirting with the gentle slopes of the San Gabriel Mountains. Raw joy floods my veins.

"Ten o'clock!" Sani shouts.

There's a shallow river surrounded by a flat area of scrubby, rocky ground ahead and to my left. I change course and slow my speed. Sensing Sani's anticipation, I fly directly over the gurgling water. Four feet press against my scales, then lift away from me. He splashes so loudly in the small river that I know he's trying to get my attention. Human or dragon, Sani only makes this much noise when it's on purpose.

I flip a quick U-turn and find him rolling in eighteen inches of water, kicking with his feet and thrashing with his tail. Childlike happiness flows from him and showers me along with the water droplets he sends spraying into the air. He flicks his tail and sends a fan of water at my face. I blink hard and laugh. Two can play this game. My tail whips around and slaps the jostling surface inches away from his smooth, satiny hide. He darts back, then jumps over the veritable tidal wave of river water.

"No fair," he says, his eyes dancing with mirth. "Your tail's so much bigger than mine."

"No fair," I echo. "Your dodge is so much faster than

mine."

His boisterous laugh fades into the darkness as he grows still, gazing at me. Warmth spreads from my center through my entire body, rushing along the spines on my back to the tips of the comb on my head and the sharp tip of my tail.

"You are so very beautiful," he says.

As he prowls toward me, I feel weak and strong at the same time. My grip on the magnetic fields falters and I drop all four feet into the water, clawed feet gripping smooth, hard river rocks.

I am swamped by the emotion rolling off Sani, thick and heavy after years of suppression. It's one—albeit an amazing and wonderful—thing for a person to say they care about you. It's entirely another animal when you can feel it; when you can know to your soul's very core the depth and breadth of every sentiment. His catlike head stretches up to mine, nuzzling his soft, feathery cheek against my leathery one.

Sani has opened the floodgates, allowing me to sense everything. As much as it terrifies me, I repay the openness. Everything I've felt for him over the past three years comes rushing out of me.

We stand inside a storm of passion and affection and love. Incapable of moving, barely capable of breathing, I'm a frozen statue, the water rushing around my feet and sweeping all my doubts and fears downstream.

Sani changes first. The soft bristle of his human hair tickles my nose. He grins sheepishly at me. "I just want to hold you in my arms."

Though the sudden loss of his emotions swirling around me leaves me feeling anemic, I can't argue with that. I tuck the dragon away and fall into human form. The bottom of the hotel robe soaks with river water, and the current pulls it away from the lower half of my body. Smiling, Sani pulls my arms up and loops them around his neck.

He slides his left hand up my right arm, underneath the wide sleeve of the robe, to softly stroke my shoulder. Icy heat trails behind his touch, spreading across my neck and down into my belly. He reaches out with his right hand and cups my face, tracing the outline of my lips with his thumb. My lips are on fire. The butterflies in my stomach roil out of control, spinning like a tiny hurricane.

"Kitty," Sani whispers. "I'm so sorry." His voice breaks with regret that tears at my hearts.

"Sorry?" I say, confused. "What for?" Was he going to tell me we couldn't be together once my mother was free again? Did he think it wasn't worth it? Did he possibly think I would let him go, knowing what I know now? My fingers dig into his back, holding him close to me. No chance in hell.

"For waiting so long to let you know how I felt," he says. "I am so sorry I pretended like I didn't care about you."

"I get it," I mumble, my eyes focusing on his shirt collar, some of the worry leaving me. "It's okay."

"No. It's not," he says, lowering his head to catch my gaze. "But I'll never hurt you like that again. I promise. From this day on, nothing will keep me from you."

Oh Gods, I melt. Kitty Lung, the fierce, avenging dragon, annihilator of terrorist cells, America's Most Wanted, is a ridiculous, molten puddle of mushy emotions. My hearts are bound to beat right out of my chest. I certainly can't contain them.

"Not even the legendary Commander Lung?" I say, a smile playing at the corners of my lips.

"Neither of them," Sani says, answering my smile. He takes a deep breath. "Not even both of them."

I tighten my grip around his neck again and pull him closer, even as I set my lips on a crash course for his. The moment our lips touch—this defines completeness. His lips move slowly and gently against mine. Too slowly, too gently.

I slide my tongue across the seal of his lips, urging him on. I want more. I want everything. A small groan sounds in his throat and he relents. We melt into each other. And finally, finally we're kissing like I've always imagined we would, like the world might end tomorrow.

And who knows? For us, it might. But right now, I really don't care.

• • •

I wake to a gentle pressure on my left temple and smile when I realize it's courtesy of Sani's soft lips. He's lying behind me in my bed, his left arm wrapped firmly around my waist. I'm curled up against his chest, as comfortable as a cat lazing in the sunshine. His warm scent washes over me and, for a second, I'm in heaven.

A knock at the door, then it swings open. "Kitty," Dominic says. "I couldn't find Sani, he's not in his— Oh!"

"What the hell!" I blink angrily at him. "I did not say you could come in."

"Good morning, Dominic," Sani says. I hear the smile in his voice and it warms me to my core.

"Well, I'm so glad you two found time to screw around before our big day."

Sani pulls slightly away from me. "We didn't, uh, screw—"

"Whatever, I don't need to know the details," Dominic says. "I hope you're both ready. Considering CNN has announced Director Bean is being held against his will, we might have a bigger fight than we bargained for."

"He didn't sound like he was being watched when I talked to him." I scramble out of bed. I'm fully clothed, despite Dominic's insinuations. I blink and stretch languidly, my body refusing to start up any faster. Sleep had come so easily with Sani's arms around me and my sleep-starved brain is in no hurry to wake. Rather, it begs me to crawl back into bed with him and pull the covers over both our heads, ignoring the rest of the world.

Dominic shrugs. "They're claiming he was taken prisoner by an *unnamed* criminal organization."

"That's actually better," Sani says. He's somehow already out of bed, looking like he's slept for a week and staring at a random spot on the wall, his mind working.

"How do you figure?" Dominic is fiddling with his belt. I notice his hand keeps moving to adjust his gun holster, which isn't there.

I smile, remembering a discussion Sani and I had last night. "He's right. It means we'll just be fighting against the Yakuza and not whatever allies Bean's managed to scrounge up. If he's there voluntarily, who knows what kind of spooks from his past he'd have helping him out." Oddly, a great weight seems to lift from me. Facing down Director Bean's dark past wasn't exactly on my bucket list.

Without answering, Dominic walks out of the room, not bothering to close the door behind him. "Get ready, lovebirds. I'm going to make the phone call. We leave in ten."

Chapter Eighteen

I swoop onto the street with dragon-form Sani riding on my back, both of us invisible to the men patrolling the roof and guarding the entrances. I take a deep breath, reveling in the last few seconds of invisibility. I am very comfortable sneaking into a place unseen and doing my job. This strategy of making sure as many people as possible see me doesn't sit well with my years of training and familiar caution. This—the moment I break all the rules—is the moment that will make or break the dragons. The blood pumping through my veins turns to ice. It seemed like such a great idea from the safety of the high-rise hotel room in the comfort of plush carpet and fancy furniture. Now, hovering a few feet from a mob stronghold? Not so much.

"Do you sense that?" Sani asks.

I listen closely to the air around us. Idle chatter from the guards and the subtle sounds of a city waking up fill my ears. Nothing out of the ordinary. "No, I don't think so."

"Inside the building," he insists. "You don't feel anything?" Sani's always trying to get me to become more observant, like a parent telling a child to look up a word in the dictionary rather than giving him the easy answer.

Opening up my senses a little more and stretching them out through the entire building, I hold my breath. At first, everything is painfully mundane—air conditioners, water flowing through pipes, steady footsteps. Then, the emotions drift up to me out of the other noises and smells. I feel a quiet, muddled mixture of uneasiness, resolution, and just a touch of fear. Oh. My. Gods. "There's a dragon in there!"

Sani's claws flex against my scales as he stiffens now that I've confirmed it. He doesn't want me to know it, but this worries him. "I wonder if it's anyone we know?"

I don't blame him for worrying. Either the Yakuza are holding a dragon hostage, in addition to Jacob and Director Bean, or a dragon is helping them. I'm not even sure which I'd prefer, but I know one thing for sure: we will not win this fight if a dragon's added himself to our opponent list.

Dominic rounds the corner, and I can't help but grin. I know seeing him has never produced this reaction in me before, but his homeless getup and drunken stumble is kind of hilarious. This is our signal; it's go time. There's no turning back, even with our newest discovery.

"Hold on," I warn Sani.

At my greatest speed, we shoot to the top of the building, and I quietly circle around the door that leads from the roof to inside. In a flash of kismet, the door hangs partially open, like it's waiting for us. The guards constantly focus their attention outward and downward, so they don't spot human-form Sani when he leaps from my back. His backpack is half full and fastened tightly to his back with chest and waist straps. He somehow manages to skulk across the gravelly roof and slip into the shadowed opening without making even the smallest of sounds.

As soon as he's out of sight behind the door, I take a deep breath. This is it. Batting down every day of training I've ever had, silencing every lecture my mother's ever given me, I release my invisibility and let loose a roar that vibrates the windows of the Yakuza building and all the buildings around us. The guards on the roof spin to face the sound. Many of them stumble at the sight of my thirty-foot-long serpentine body circling and darting like a crazed moth around a light bulb. One screams and dives behind an air conditioning unit.

I give them enough time to get a good look, but not enough to train their weapons on me. I soar straight up into the sky and circle out of pistol range, keeping an eye on Dominic on the street below.

He's been obnoxious enough to draw the attention of most of the street guards, excluding those who are still searching the sky looking for the source of my earth-shaking roar. I knew I gave him a job perfectly suited to his skills; he's remarkably excellent at annoying people. I keep my eyes on him. Yeah, the drunk hobo act is a great diversion, but its true purpose is to give me a sign I can see from this high up in the sky.

It's only a few seconds longer until he trips over his own feet and flails on the ground, the prearranged signal. The signal does double duty, drawing attention away from the building just as Sani reaches the bottom and opens the cargo door on that side of the building.

I dive, pushing the magnetic currents around me to fall even faster than gravity would allow. On the way down, I spot a perfectly primped woman with a cameraman setting up on the roof of the next building over. It looks like our media guests have arrived, just on time. One thing you can always count on the media for is being willing to receive an exclusive on the biggest story of the year.

At the last second before crashing into the pavement, I pull up and speed down the sidewalk, knocking stunned Yakuza guards over with my thrashing tail. When I reach the end of the building, I spin in a barely controlled U-turn and make a second pass. The guards who survived the first run-through now have guns in their hands.

The sting of a bullet rips through muscle in my midsection. I roar as I knock the shooter to the ground with a swipe of my head. Blood trickles from his forehead. He doesn't move again.

The bullet went in at an angle, but takes the shortest possible path out of my muscle, tearing another gash through my side. I grit my teeth as a few drops of my blood splatter on the yellow dividing line on the street, followed by the ding of a spent bullet on the pavement.

Dominic has recovered from his feigned drunken stupor. He's just to the side of the open cargo door, knocking out the occasional man who runs out of it with a rusty pipe he must have found on the street. I still wasn't comfortable with him having a gun, even though having one more offensive ally would have made things easier. But if the kitsune shows up, he would swiftly turn from ally to one more obstacle. And, as much as I hate to admit it, he's not a weak enemy.

One last guard remains standing on the street. I know more can't be far away; I've made one hell of a racket. I fly full speed at him. Bullets zip past my head. One nicks my foot, but the injury will heal in seconds. I swerve just before I crash into him and whip my tail around, sending him flying into the wall of the building across the street. His gun clatters to the sidewalk. Dominic stares at it, contemplating. My dragon rages, more in control of me than I've allowed in a very long time. I roar at him and he backs away.

"Gotcha," he says, holding up his hands in surrender.

I shake my head, trying to wrestle control from the dragon. She's stronger and faster than me, but she's even more unpredictable than I am. I need control to pull this off.

Asphalt explodes just to my left. And then closer, on my right. I had almost forgotten about the guards on the roof. Bullets rain down on the street. Dominic ducks into the relative safety of the Yakuza warehouse, and I am seconds behind him. You know it's an interesting day when you consider leaping into a mob warehouse "safety."

The room we enter spans the entire footprint of the building with a polished concrete floor. Four metal staircases climb at random intervals along the exterior walls, leading to upper levels hidden from view. The dragon we sensed earlier is on another floor, a few stories up.

The left half of the room is occupied by vehicles of all shapes and sizes: Hummers, sports cars, ghetto jalopies, SUVs, delivery trucks, even motorcycles. I'm sure they all have proper paperwork. The right wall is lined by huge mysteriously unlabeled wooden crates and endless rows of metal cabinets. Hmm, I wonder what *those* could hold. I doubt it's cleaning supplies.

The rest of the room is home to a jumbled assortment of furniture. Picnic tables, couches, folding chairs, and cafeteria tables with mismatched chairs lie empty and quiet. Bottles, cans, and decks of playing cards litter the tables. I picture dozens of Yakuza thugs and hopefuls lounging here later in the day, waiting for action. Yeah, striking in the morning was definitely a good call. Though I didn't expect the first floor to be quite *this* empty. There's not a soul in sight.

Including Sani.

He was supposed to wait for me in here, keeping an eye out for any major danger. It's way too early for him to be deviating from the plan already. Something has to have pulled him away. Could it have been the dragon? The kitsune? Gods, I hope it's just a human with a big gun. Maybe he found a way to draw away any guards from this floor to give me more time.

The cars are a welcome sight, though.

I nod at Dominic and point at the collection with the tip of my tail. "Can you hotwire a car?"

"Of course," he says, sounding hurt.

"Start up that Hummer and keep it warm for us, just in case. Stay low. You can keep a better eye on the door from inside there than you can out in the open."

He nods once, scanning the room. "Where's Sani?"

"Upstairs," I say.

His brows crease as he glances at the ceiling. "Why?"

"I don't know." My stomach tightens. "But I can sense him. He's alive and not afraid, at the very least. If we're not back in fifteen, you get out of here."

I fly up the closest staircase, but have to switch back to human form to open and fit through the door at the top. My backpack rematerializes on my back along with my clothes. I reach back and slip out a pistol. The wound on my stomach hurts a hell of a lot more in this form, but it's nothing I haven't worked through before. The bullet's already been rejected and the tissue is trying to knit together—if I would just stop moving long enough for it to heal, I'd be golden.

I place my left hand on the doorknob and pause a second to listen. I don't hear a thing on the other side of the metal door, but that doesn't necessarily mean it's empty. Who knows what kind of setup the mob has here. There's got to be at least one safe room. I crouch low, making myself a very small target, and inch the door open.

I scooch through the door, my pistol leading the way.

I enter a room that looks exactly like any other cubicle farm at any business in the country. No signs of life appear, but I make my way through the room, clearing it one cubicle at a time. At the end of the fourth and final row, there is a manager's office. The door is shut, but I can see slices of a desk and chair through the partially closed blinds. I need to clear this room too, just in case Jacob is inside, mouth taped shut and tied to a chair or something. I wouldn't put it past the Yakuza to be so cliché.

I place my back against the wall next to the door and slowly turn the knob. Pushing the door open with my elbow, I sweep into the room, gun at the ready.

Nothing. Silence. Breath stored for too long whooshes out of my lungs.

A desk with papers scattered across it, a dusty monitor, a dirty coffee cup. No Jacob, though. And no Yakuza. I'm just about to run back to the warehouse's main entrance when a bright pink square of paper catches my eye.

KL is written in big bold letters. Underneath, my Secret Service phone number is written in perfect, feminine handwriting. Something about the way the six curls in on itself scratches at my brain.

I rush to the desk and crumple the paper in my hand. I'll make sure to tell my Secret Service contact about this massive security breach—if I make it out of this building alive. I scan the other papers on the desk.

The rest of them are written in neat Japanese script, which I can't read. I do recognize a drawing, though. It's the layout of the Academy and surrounding streets. I unsnap the straps of my backpack and shrug it off. I don't have time to figure out what this means now, but I scoop all the papers into my hands and shove them in the pack. It's too full so I choose a pistol to sacrifice to make room for the papers and leave it on the desk. I figure the Yakuza have enough guns; one more isn't going to make a difference.

I run back to the warehouse, strapping on the backpack. As soon as I burst out of the door at the top of the staircase, I leap into the air and snap to my dragon form before I lose any altitude. I sense the steely calm that comes over Sani when he's in a fight. He's close and he's not alone. I fly to the next staircase over and change back to the five-foot-four version of Kitty Lung. I don't have to stop and listen this time to hear the chaos on the other side of this door. Grunts, curses, and the undeniable sound of bodies crashing into hard things.

I throw the door open and tuck into a ball at the same time. I roll into the room and stop in a squat, my gun pointing forward. I have no idea what this room used to be used for, but now it looks like a doctor's exam room that's recently housed a tornado. Metal trays and instruments scatter across the floor.

Sani, in his sleek black dragon form, circles across from a creature that resembles a humanized cartoonish fox, like from the animated Robin Hood series. They take swipes at each other so quickly my eyes can't follow the movement, but I don't hear bodily contact.

I aim my gun at the fox thing. I can only assume it's the kitsune after losing all control over her glamor. Unarmed Japanese men lie scattered around the room in various states of injury and consciousness. Who knows how long Sani's been fighting this creature and her lackeys? I can't figure out why she doesn't put him in a haze like she did with me. Maybe it's not just her glamor she loses control of when she's flustered. Or maybe she hasn't been able to lay a hand on him yet.

She's perfectly in my line of fire. I squeeze the trigger. In the same instant, she lunges toward Sani and he spins to avoid her attack. The bullet whizzes by, inches away from his black catlike head. Okay, so I won't try that again.

"Kitty!" Sani huffs out between breaths, blows, and blocks. "Find Jacob. Meet…you at…rendezvous."

I know I should do as he says. As in, right away. But I hesitate. The two seem evenly matched—and she has help. Dark red blood sprays out from several wounds along the length of his salamander-like body with every move. Dark, wet spots on the kitsune's fur give me a smidgeon of comfort. Though they may simply keep on giving each other paper cuts until they both fall into tiny pieces.

Even as I consider staying to help him, I know this is why partners aren't supposed to be involved. Wanting to stay goes against every second of training I've ever had. But leaving him goes against every fiber of my being. The memory of his green eyes, staring into mine like he never wanted to look at anything else, flashes through my head. I take half a step toward the swirling melee.

"Go!" Sani yells. "Now!"

Before I have time to decide against it, I turn and dive out of the door. I hop once on the top of the stairs and back into the air, shifting mid-leap. Only two staircases left.

The third door is quiet, so I sneak in in human form, gun poised for action. What I see reminds me of our dorm hallways at DIC, long and featureless with many identical and symmetrical doors. Except there are three heavily armed Yakuza guards standing in front of one of the doors at the end of the hallway.

Bingo.

They spot me. This hallway is just wide enough for my dragon form, so I shift. Then roar. And promptly disappear.

A confused enemy is an easily defeated enemy. That's the idea, anyway. My dragon urges me to rush them and swallow them whole, but I hold on enough to my humanity to realize how terrible an idea that would be.

However, these three guards seem to be ready for my bag of tricks. In synch, they drop down to one knee and begin firing at my last known location. I press myself against the left wall, but a bullet rips through my right rear leg. Then another finds a home in my tail.

Crap. I am too big of a fish in too small of a barrel. Soon I'll look like Swiss cheese. I drop the invisibility, then shift. A bullet lodges into the wall right where my dragon-head just was.

Now I'm a much smaller target. A weaker, slower target, but smaller.

The gun is still in my right hand. I kick in the door to my left and put a little concrete and steel between me and the armed guards. Two spent, blood-coated bullets clang to the ground. There's a generous tear in my right calf muscle from the first, closing up even as I examine it. A burning sensation in my right butt cheek lets me know the location of the second.

I try to stand straight, but my right leg protests in agony. I won't be rushing these guys in human form, that's for sure. I fire blind around the corner into the hallway. Seven shots. I hear the satisfying thunk of a bullet burying in human flesh in between shots.

Two guns continue to fire. One doesn't. I like these odds a little better. But I'll never hit both of them, firing blind. I'm fully in the room now, but they continue to fire down the hallway. They know my invisibility trick and aren't ready to risk an ambush.

I take a quick look around the room. My first impression was correct. These are definitely dorms for the troops. But these guys have to share a room with bunk beds—and cheaply-constructed ones at that. Suckers.

Then I realize something else. The room is big enough for me to shift. I can't rush the hallway invisible and risk they'll hit one of my hearts—because then none of us would escape this place alive. But I just need a look so I know where to aim.

I sigh. All this shifting is going to make me feel like crap tonight. I will actually have to eat a whole cow. Maybe two.

I shift again, go invisible, and poke as little of my dragon head as possible into the hall. I keep it high against the ceiling, where they're not concentrating their fire right now.

I memorize their locations, pull my head back in and snap back to human form. The quick changes are getting to me. I'm a little dizzy this time around, and my vision blurs.

As soon as I can see straight again, I fire four quick shots down the hall, two at each location. Another thunk and a thud. One gun's still firing, though.

Holy crap, how many rounds does this guy have? I knew I should have spent more time learning about guns. I'll apologize to Simon as soon as I get out of this, I promise. Then I'll study until I know all of it—not just enough to pass the examinations. It's funny the prayers and promises you make in situations like this.

I see a small puddle of blood below me; maybe the dizziness isn't completely due to the shifts.

I take deep breaths, steadying my spinning head. Two more shifts and I'll have him. Two more, I can totally do this.

Dragon form. I feel so much stronger like this, not dizzy at all. But I can't fire a gun with my giant claws. And I really can't risk this Yakuza firing crazily and randomly down the hallway, hitting one of my hearts. We *have to* fly out of here. I peek out into the hallway.

The bastard's using his two fallen comrades as a shield. He's lying down on the ground behind them, using the second's shoulder to steady his shots.

His head is completely in the open, though. I linger in the doorway, memorizing his location, visualizing my next shot firing true into the middle of his forehead. Gods forgive me, I hate using guns. They're hands-down the worst human invention, next to the nuclear bomb. And maybe reality television. But it's Jacob or these guys, and that's not a difficult decision to make.

I pull my head back in and snap to human form. The dorm room spins around me. I sway and lean against the wall. I give myself three slow, strong breaths. One. Two. Three.

My hand snakes around the corner and fires a single shot. The semiautomatic gunfire ceases. I force two quick breaths and peek quickly around the corner—in human form; I'm not sure I can change again. The image of that man's face, with a red dot in the middle of his forehead, a trickle of blood dripping on his fallen colleague, will haunt me for years.

Yeah, I know he was a mob guy. I know he was destined for a violent death. I just didn't want to be the one to deliver it.

I'm leaning heavily against the wall. Bullet wounds, though healing, still bleed on my stomach, right calf, and butt. I stare at the lower bunk bed for a few seconds, wishing more than anything I could lie down on it—just for a few minutes.

But I know I can't. I *know* it. If I lie down, I may never get back up. I just have to convince myself of it. Funny how that works, huh?

I drop the gun on the floor. I never want to see it again. But I'm not an idiot: I have more in my pack if I need them. I limp down the hallway, leaning against the left wall for support. A calf muscle is one of those you never really think about until it doesn't work anymore. It shortens my stride by half and sends shooting pains through my lower leg if I stretch too far. I finally reach the door the three Yakuza were guarding and turn the handle.

Well, I *try* to turn the handle. But it doesn't budge. Have I forgotten how to turn a door handle? I stare at it for a few seconds until the explanation slogs its way through my muddled brain: locked. Tired and weary, my dragon roars inside my head.

"Are you freaking kidding me?" I shout at no one in particular.

"Kitty?" a small, familiar voice sounds on the other side of the door.

"Jacob?" I call. "Jacob!" I bang against the door. Just hearing his voice renews my strength. My dragon, programmed to the max to protect this boy, urges to the surface. We are so close. So close.

"Can you move in the room?" I ask.

"Yeah," he says. "It locks from the outside, with a key."

I glance at the fallen Yakuza. Their blood seeps to the ground and swirls together in a shallow pool of crimson against the stark white of the linoleum floor. I really don't want to search all of them for a key they may not have.

"Get as far from the door as you can, to the side," I say. "Put some furniture between you and it if you can." I pick up the last Yakuza's gun, which has fallen to the floor a few feet away from him and mercifully doesn't have any blood on it.

"Okay," he says, sounding more distant. "I'm ready."

I squeeze the trigger once and three fast shots make scrap metal out of the door lock. Hell, no wonder these guys were tearing me up. Why don't I have guns like this? My dad and I are going to have a little chat about his armory once he's free. I throw my shoulder against the door, and it swings open, banging against the wall. This room looks exactly the same as the other one. Jacob is crouching behind a wooden dresser, looking more terrified than I've ever seen him.

"Kitty! You're hurt!" Jacob rushes to my side and slides under my shoulder to support some of my weight. He leads me to the lower bunk and helps me to sit down. Without another word, he tears strips of fabric from the bedsheets and gently wraps my calf. His fingers shake, but he's careful to avoid touching my injury. He bites his lip as he focuses on the task.

Gods help me, I want to cry. Ignoring the politics surrounding it, I know with both of my hearts that rescuing this kid was the right thing to do.

He looks at the blood staining the shirt over my stomach. "Should I wrap that, too?"

"Don't worry about it," I say. "It's almost healed."

"Almost healed?" His eyebrows scrunch together as he stares at the stain. "The blood looks fresh."

"Yeah, uh. I'm going to have to make this quick, but how much have they told you about what's going on?"

"Nothing. Like, nothing at all. I've only seen Gesina and this big scary-looking man with gray eyes since I've been here. What's going on, Kitty? Tell me the truth this time, please." His words come spilling out of his mouth, fueled by fear and confusion.

"All right." I take a deep breath. Then another. I move to stand at the door, still clutching the Yakuza's gun, scanning for sounds of anyone entering the dorm hallway. I have to lean against the doorjamb more heavily than I'd like. "*Reader's Digest* summary? I'm a sort of human-dragon shape-shifter. So is Sani. We're rescuing you now, along with Agent Dominic Harris. And we have to be seen doing it so that we can maybe get all of the other people like us released from CIA's custody."

"Whoa." Surprise, but not disbelief. He's been waiting a long time for the truth.

"Oh yeah, and Gesina is an evil Japanese fox woman creature thing."

"Whoa."

I can't help but laugh. "I know, right?"

"You're a freaking dragon?" His eyes go wide and he looks me over like he might see something dragonish about me.

"Yeah, so is Sani."

"Can I see?"

My head swims at the thought of changing. I groan. "Please, not right now."

"Later, you promise?"

"Definitely. First, we need to find Sani and get the hell out of here before the Yakuza can regroup."

Chapter Nineteen

I give myself three minutes—no more, despite Jacob's protests—to rest and to heal. I've downed a bottle of water and a candy bar Jacob had in his room and I'm feeling almost alive. My brain feels like it's spinning inside my head, but at least I can stand without stumbling. We're walking to the stairway when the door leading downstairs swings open. I stop and shove Jacob behind me, wishing I'd kept that gun in my hand. I'm not sure how many more times I can change without passing the heck out but I let my dragon hover close to the surface, just in case.

Who steps through that door but Director Bean himself, looking as fierce and in control as ever. His suit is perfect, his hair pristine.

Jacob ducks behind my back. "That's the scary gray-eyed man," he whispers.

"No kidding," I whisper back. I meet the aforementioned eyes and do my very best not to flinch away from them.

"What are you doing here, Ms. Lung?" Director Bean's voice is rife with disapproval.

Jacob grabs my left elbow. "You know him?" he hisses in my ear.

I ignore Jacob, but answer the director. "I'm rescuing you, sir," I say with as much authority as I can conjure up.

"Are you?" He laughs. "What gave you the impression I needed rescuing?"

I try to keep the fear out of my voice, but I think it trembles a little when I say, "CNN."

"Oh good," he says, a cocky smirk flashing across his face. "I'm so glad those old guys pulled through for me. I've called in too many favors the last week."

"Is that Kitty?" a female voice from the other side of the door says.

Director Bean flashes a frown over his shoulder. "I told you to wait until I was sure it was safe."

Marcy appears in the doorway. She's abandoned her usual sharp business suit for a green, flowy, strapless dress that accentuates her curves and beautifully complements the patches of dragon skin on her face and arms. I've always thought she was pretty, but, right now, she's absolutely gorgeous. Neither of them look like they're being held against their will. So if she wasn't taken, how did she escape the internment? Marcy hadn't left DIC compound since her accident, so there's no way she simply lucked out like Sani and I had. Marcy must have been the dragon Sani and I were sensing earlier—but my muddled brain couldn't figure out why she'd be here, of all places. Suddenly, the familiar curl of the six in my phone number on the Post-it note makes sense. I've received hundreds of notes from Marcy over the years.

I really should've recognized her handwriting.

"John, you told me she wouldn't be involved," she says. John?

"I tried, dear," he says, placing an arm around her waist.

Dear? Oh man, I *knew* they had something going on!

"So you did orchestrate all this," I say, nodding, pretending like I have everything figured out. "It smelled like you. Though I never figured you for a traitor to your country." What I do not have to pretend is the disgust that leaks its way into my words.

"I did it for you." Director Bean shrugs.

"For the dragons," Marcy corrects. She slips her arm through his and smiles up at him. My stomach turns. "For all of us."

Director Bean smiles warmly down at her and touches her hand with his before returning his gaze back to me. "Like I told the president, if he releases the dragons, his son will be returned completely unharmed."

"Not that we planned on harming Jacob either way," Marcy adds in a hurry.

Wait, what? Releasing the dragons does not equal nuclear launch codes.

"You spoke to the president directly?" I ask, rage slowly seething into my consciousness, my dragon braying inside my head in response.

"Well, I'm not an idiot—I used a voice synthesizer and bounced the signal off about a hundred satellites. But yes, I spoke to him."

Someone has lied to us. Probably many someones. And I don't think Director Bean is playing me, at least not right now. So that only leaves one particular Head of State.

"And you told him you'd release Jacob if..." I trail off, wanting him to confirm it, to say it again so I can make sure I'm hearing this right.

"Well, it's a little complicated, but, essentially the deal was this: Jacob's freedom in exchange for all dragonkind's freedom." Bean's voice is calm, cool, and matter-of-fact.

Mine, on the other hand...

"That rat-bastard sack of lying crap!" I yell. I point at Jacob. "I am going to kick your father in the nuts! Twice!"

"I think that may be considered treason," Jacob mumbles, not quite understanding what we're talking about. His eyes dart back and forth between the three of us, but I think he's still too terrified of Bean to ask any questions.

Director Bean smirks. "What did he tell you? I'm assuming terrorism was involved?" His aplomb grates against my nerves like sandpaper.

"Forty-eight hours. Nuclear launch codes," I say through clenched teeth.

He laughs like we're all at a cocktail party, and someone just told a joke. "Is he getting his lies from summer action movies now?"

I mutter for about a minute, using no less than thirty-five words my mother would slap me for uttering. The whole time, Bean is smirking at me, his eyes laughing at my idiocy. I fell for the president's story, hook, line, and sinker. I didn't even doubt it for a second and the whole thing had been a lie. Give the damn man an Oscar to go with his presidency. Hell, give him all the awards. It will make it that much sweeter when I strip everything from him.

I meet Bean's eyes and raise an eyebrow. "How do I know you're not lying?" I ask Bean, not wanting to get duped again. I wouldn't put it past the man to pull a double—or even triple—cross.

Jacob clears his throat. "I don't know about the rest, but I heard the call he made to my father. Once the 'subjects'"— he makes air quotes around the word—"were declared free and equal, I'd be delivered safely to the White House's front door."

"That dirty rotten no-good lump of camel shit!" I want to punch something and feel it break underneath my fist. If there is anything I hate more than being lied to, it is falling for the lies.

"You still sure you want to rescue this one, then?" Director Bean asks, pointing at Jacob.

"Now, wait a minute!" Jacob says. "Whatever my dad did—"

I place a reassuring hand on his shoulder and answer the director. "Yes. Luckily, our plan ensures the president will end up with egg on his face. And your buddies at CNN spreading the news that you're being held against your will only helps us."

"Well," Director Bean rises onto his toes and something unrecognizable flashes across his face. "That's actually not a complete lie, exactly."

My mouth hangs open. "What, *exactly*, do you *actually* mean?"

Marcy steps forward, quiet, but commanding attention. "When we arrived here, we discovered the Yakuza had a plan that differed from the original."

"The kitsune had different plans," Bean amends. "They just do what she tells them, the little sorceress."

Now I recognize the strange look that had crossed Bean's face earlier. For the first time since I've met him, the director is not in absolute command.

"You planned all this!" I say. "You told me to not to come here."

"I...uh..." he begins.

Marcy's clipped, clear voice sums everything up. "We've lost control of the situation. We've been going along with them for now, looking for an opportunity to get Jacob out."

A sly grin curls up one side of my mouth. I can't help it. "You needed me to rescue you."

Director Bean stands straighter and raises his chin. "We are running out of time. She's here. What's your extraction plan?"

Properly intimidated, I explain the rest of the plan to Director Bean. Marcy and Jacob listen intently.

"Ballsy," he says when I'm done. I think it's the nicest thing he's ever said to me and I almost smile at him. But then I remember who I'm talking to.

"Well..." I gesture toward myself in a you-know-me kind of way. "I am a Lung, after all."

"A burned spy fighting a war in the court of public opinion." Director Bean laughs. "There's something poetic about that."

"I don't know anything about poetry. But I do know that people believe *anything* this guy tells them," I say, pointing at Jacob. A bitter thought invades my thoughts. "Just like his father, apparently. What do you say, Midday Sun? Will you help us?"

He taps his chin like he's considering it. "If I do, you'll give me an aerial tour of D.C.?"

Figures, he was just considering what he could get out of it. But I'm more than okay with this sort of trade.

"Sure," I say. "If it works."

What I don't say: if it doesn't work, I won't be giving an aerial tour of anything to anybody ever again, not even myself.

"Let's do it," Jacob says.

. . .

When we return to the first floor of the warehouse, Dominic is pacing circles around the Hummer. His shoulders are squeezed in tight and I can hear his jaw clenching from all the way across the cavernous space.

"I told you to stay out of sight," I say. "What are you doing?"

"That girl," he says, panic making his breaths come fast. "The pretty German one. She has Sani. She wants you up on the roof, or she said she'll kill him. She has, like, twenty Yakuza with her."

I close my eyes. The kitsune has Sani. Breathe in. Breathe out.

"Sani said for you not to do it," Dominic adds. "He said get out, get Jacob to safety." There's a weight to his words that I can't figure out with everyone's pulse drumming in my ears.

"Of course he did. All right, you take the Hummer and get them out of here." I motion to Director Bean, Marcy, and Jacob. "Lose whatever tail may follow you. I'll meet you at the rendezvous in two hours."

I head for the fourth staircase, the only one I haven't explored yet, so it must be the one that leads to the roof. I breathe in and out again, slowly, trying to keep the dragon from bursting out of me. She thunders in my head, but stays beneath my thin layer of control.

"Uh, Kitty," Dominic says, damaging my calm.

I whirl to face him. "What!" A bass note runs through the word, rumbling just below the surface of it.

He ducks his head. "She also said she'll kill Sani if Jacob leaves."

I'm going to tear this girl into tiny little pieces and then scatter those pieces across the ocean. Risking my life for Sani's? No big deal. But risking Jacob's? No dice. "Jacob's the primary concern," I say. "Get him out of here."

"No," Jacob says. He runs to stand beside me, head held high in defiance.

"Jacob, get in the car," I growl.

"No," he repeats. "Sani's risked his life for me. I'm not going to leave if it means he gets killed. Plus, you need to be seen rescuing me if your plan is going to work, if you want to free your parents."

I recognize the determination in his eyes, and I don't have time to argue. "Okay," I say. "But you don't go up on the roof. You stay one level below."

"Then I go with you," Dominic says, stepping up next to Jacob. He's still a Secret Service agent, assigned to Jacob. I'd expect nothing less.

"And I'll go with you," Director Bean says to me.

Now that surprises me. I raise my eyebrow at him, but before I get the chance to question him, Marcy speaks.

"Me too!" she says. Her eyes are bright with excitement and danger.

I sigh, looking at all of them. My life would be so much simpler if these people were more selfish. Arguing with them is going to get me nowhere except further into the kitsune's bad graces for delaying my answer to her summons. I pull a gun out of my pack and hand it to Marcy. "Marcy's with me.

The rest of you will stay with Jacob."

A chorus of three male voices rises up in protest.

"Look, I'd rather not have to shoot you guys. You're all human, which means the kitsune can play you like puppets. You *will* stay below."

A grumbling chorus of agreement answers me. They don't like it, but even Director Bean recognizes his weakness against the manipulative creature.

We jog up the last staircase. It simply leads to another staircase, then another. Finally, I find a door that says ROOF.

I turn to the four people behind me. "Marcy, hide your weapon unless it's needed. Stay low. Do not let her touch you." Marcy nods and tucks the pistol somewhere near her thigh, underneath the flowing dress. A pang of guilt passes through my hearts. She looks like a kindergarten teacher, not a warrior. I know she was once a soldier, but it's been a long time. And she's just so freaking sweet.

"Guys," I say. "Stay behind this door until I call you. No matter what else you hear, do not come out. She has to see your eyes to control you." I think, anyway.

They all nod reluctantly.

"I mean it!" I whisper-shout. "Do not make me shoot you. I will do it."

"Oh, I believe you," Dominic says.

"Okay," I say, taking a deep breath. "Here goes."

I burst out onto the rooftop. Marcy follows behind me like a mouse.

This is not an ideal tactical situation. Armed Yakuza line the perimeter of the roof. The air buzzes with an intangible energy. The kitsune stands at the edge of the roof next to Sani, who is bound at the ankles, wrists, and shoulders. He's standing on the very edge of the roof, centimeters from the edge.

"Kitty." How can he sound so angry? I came here to rescue him. "You should have left."

"Oh good," the kitsune, once again dressed in a photoshopped version of Gesina's skin, purrs. Do foxes purr? Kitsune definitely do. "I was afraid I was going to have to dispose of this fine specimen." She runs her hand slowly across Sani's bicep like she's admiring an expensive car.

I'm going to tear all of that pretty hair from her pretty little head and feed it to her. A cool breeze washes across the rooftop, blowing hair into my eyes. It feels like ice sliding along my skin.

I dart toward her. She places a firmer hand on Sani's shoulder and tsk's her tongue. I swear to myself: I will break every single finger she uses to touch him. "No, no, no," she says. "One more step and I'll push him."

"He can survive that fall," I say.

"Ten stories? Maybe in dragon form—but…" She waves her arms up and down like Vanna White showing off a puzzle. "One graze of the skin and he won't even remember what a dragon is. You remember how it feels, right?"

My dragon growls. Because she's right. Incapacitated by her sorcery, he may survive the fall, but he may not. Sixty-forty, at best. I can't take that chance, not with Sani. I meet his eyes for a second. My entire body aches to run toward him, to grab him and fly away to our own little private island in the South Pacific. To leave all of this behind us and just be. But that's not a life either of us could live with.

"What do you want?" I yell.

"Kitty," Sani yells over us. "Leave!"

"What I've always wanted," she says. "You."

What the what? My hearts hammer in response to this strange declaration. "Why me?" I say. Who the hell am I?

"I wouldn't have taken this job if it weren't for you. Like one point two million is enough to hire a kitsune?" She sniffs the air. "It's an insult. But then I found out I'd get to play against Katherine Lung."

"Uh, yeah. Really enjoying this playtime," I say, wheels spinning in my head. Do I know her somehow? "You still didn't answer the question. Why me?"

"Cairo. 1997. Ring a bell?" Her voice drips with fire and ice.

The Cairo job. The job where a mercenary kitsune turned on the dragons and tried to kill my father. The job where my mother destroyed the kitsune who tried.

"Ah, I see it does." Her voice bites at my skin. "Your mother killed my mother. Now, it's time for payback."

This girl has a surreally warped sense of justice. Her hand clenches around Sani's shoulder, and he winces. She's hurting him. I have to get her to forget about him and focus on me.

"Hey! Your mother tried to kill my father first."

"Yeah, but she didn't, did she? He's alive and well."

We have two very different definitions of "well." "So you want me because my mother is more *effective* than yours? You're telling me you played along with this whole thing just to get at me?"

"Well, that, and to see your government squirm around like a bunch of ants someone just poured water on." She giggles like a child playing in a sandbox.

This girl is seriously twisted. I have to get control of the situation. And fast. I do the math: a two-hundred pound man will take about two point five seconds to fall ten stories. Two point five seconds. That's cutting it close.

"Okay, well," I say, shrugging. "It's been great reminiscing, but I think I'll be going now." I turn around. I don't even know where I find the self-control to pretend like I don't care what will happen to Sani. Maybe my father lent me some along with the guns.

"No!" the kitsune yells, her German accent slipping into a soft Japanese one. I hear her heart quicken to a frenzy. Any time now.

I keep walking until I hear the sound of Sani's feet slipping on concrete. The Yakuza soldiers already lean toward that edge, ready to watch him fall. I leap into the air and back flip three times across the length of the roof. The fourth back flip sends me sailing into the kitsune, knocking us both off the roof. I think my therapist might have something to say about how jumping off a roof is my definition of gaining control of a situation.

Airborne, I kick the kitsune in her gut before she has a chance to voodoo me. I shift for what I hope is the second-to-last time today and propel myself toward the ground. Sani is too far away from me, bound and plummeting toward the asphalt. Two point five seconds doesn't seem like a lot of time until the love of your life is falling to his possible death just out of your reach, hours after you finally admit how you feel about him. Then, two point five seconds is an eternity.

I'm getting closer to him, but he's getting closer to splatting on the street below. His eyes are wide open, staring into mine with complete indifference. I'd be screaming my head off if the situation were reversed. She's whammied him. The strength of his stare seems to pull me closer, giving me an extra burst of speed.

With three-tenths of a second to spare I swoop underneath Sani, catching him in the coils of my dragon body. Relief floods through every fiber of my body when a fast breath escapes his mouth. Sani is alive.

The kitsune has shifted into a full-on white fox form and somehow manages to land on her feet. The tiny crack of a single bone breaking rings up and down the street. She pulls one front paw up close to her body, whimpering. Even in the tiny fox eyes, I can see the hate there. Her gaze follows me, then looks down at her broken leg. She shakes her head in disgust and scampers into a dark alley on three feet.

Chapter Twenty

I return to the roof, readying myself to help Marcy fight off half an army of mobsters. I'm expecting a war zone, but the Yakuza seem to be standing around in a confused stupor. They mutter to each other in perturbed tones and stare at me like I'm the first monster they've ever seen.

The influence of the kitsune must have fallen away from them when she made her escape. They're not looking at us like sworn enemies, but they're not really sure why we're crawling all over their turf either. I'm a fan of getting out of here before they figure it out.

I fly over to the roof door to call down to Jacob, Director Bean, and Dominic. Marcy opens the door. They're all standing just on the other side, ears pressed to an invisible plane that had been a door a second ago. Only Jacob has the decency to look guilty. At least the other two cast a concerned glance around the roof until they spot Sani and let out a collective sigh.

The guilt on Jacob's face gives way to awe. This is the first time Jacob's seen me in my dragon form, and he was kidnapped before getting to see the footage of Wallace. Like Sani says, knowing and seeing are two very different things.

"Holy shit, you're a dragon!" he says.

"I told you," I remind him.

"Yeah, but—I don't know. I thought maybe you were speaking in metaphors or something. You're an actual, flying, fire-breathing dragon."

"I don't have any fire breath."

"Oh, that sucks," Jacob says.

"Tell me about it." I sigh. It's a sore spot between me and just about every English dragon I've ever met.

Director Bean glances meaningfully around at the Yakuza men on the roof. "We should probably get out of here. They only helped and housed me because they were all under Inari's spell."

"Inari?" I ask.

Director Bean settles his unsettling gray eyes on me. "The kitsune's real name."

"Are you sure it's her real name?" I ask.

He shakes his head. "You never know with a kitsune."

So why the hell would you hire one? I don't start this argument; there's time for it later. Right now, I have a daring rescue to pull off.

"Ready for the hard part?" I ask

"Hard part?" Jacob's jaw drops. "Kitty, you have three gunshot wounds and Sani was just pushed off a building."

I shrug. "I'm not saying that was pleasant, but I'd do it three times over again if I didn't have to deal with the media."

Jacob takes a step into the sunlight and puffs out his

chest. His golden hair shines in the rays of light and his blue eyes practically glow. "Just let me do all the talking."

Gods help us.

I stretch out the length of my dragon body. "Okay, everybody on."

"There are five of us," Dominic points out.

"Ooh, guys, look who learned to count!" I coo.

"You don't have to be such a b—" He glances at Jacob before continuing "—be so mean. You said you couldn't carry both Sani and me."

"Across the country. We're just going to the next building over to make a dramatic entrance for the camera. I can make it."

I'm pretty sure, anyway.

They climb on, and I rise shakily into the air. The weight is tough enough, but it's the balancing act that has my muscles aching before we cross above the street. I pool my last reserves of energy and focus on keeping my passengers from tottering too much. Dropping the president's son a few stories on national television wouldn't do a whole lot of good for my dubious reputation.

Jacob whoops as we cross over the roof ledge of the building where the reporter waits, red light flashing on her camera.

"We made it!" he shouts, grinning at the camera lens. "I can't wait to go home."

I can't blame him for not realizing the effect his words have on the rest of our group. Sani and Marcy must be thinking the same thing I am: we have no home we can go to.

Chapter Twenty-One

Every TV station has been playing the same five minutes of film over and over for the last twenty-four hours. Me, flying from the Yakuza rooftop across to "safety," where the reporter and cameraman just happen to be. The five people might have been a little too much weight for me, but the lumbering flight path only makes for an even more dramatic image. Human-form Sani leaps to the rooftop to help Director Bean, Dominic, and Jacob disembark before I take off again. We hadn't wanted to wait around in case any CIA clowns showed up.

Jacob is perfection. He shakes and takes deep, shuddering breaths when recounting his "horrific" kidnapping, but seamlessly slides into an awed, grateful kid as he describes his rescue.

"There aren't many people who would face an armed mob for me, especially when we have her family in a cage. She took three bullets for me and kept going. She's a hero."

Maybe it's too much, but he sells it like a three in the morning infomercial. With his wide, blue eyes and strategically winking dimples, he looks like a little kid, not the sixteen-year-old charmer I know so well. There isn't a single living soul who would dare to contradict him. Or so you would think.

A stony-faced Secret Service media representative fills the screen, microphones jostling in front of him, vying for position. A harsh sun lights up half his face and casts the other half in deep shadow. This was obviously a hastily assembled press conference. "The Secret Service is collaborating with the CIA and FBI to investigate all events preceding and following Jacob's ordeal."

Yeah, I'm sure the CIA is taking an unbiased approach to the investigation.

An unseen female reporter shouts a question. "What can you tell us about the dragon who rescued him?"

I hate this part, every time. "We are making no assumptions at this time. Eyewitness accounts of the kidnapping indicate an individual with similar abilities to the dragons who committed the kidnapping in the first place."

Ugh. He didn't say it outright, but he implied it: a dragon doing the kidnapping negates a dragon doing the saving. It's not even a dragon! But can we tell the world about the kitsune? They probably won't handle the news too well, much less be able to tell the difference between us.

Sani tightens his arm around my shoulder and pulls me closer to his side, placing a gentle kiss on the top of my head. We're sitting in another fancy hotel room courtesy of Wallace and CINDY, registered to one Mary Smith, who just so happens to look exactly like Marcy, who nobody is currently hunting. She's sitting at the table in the kitchen reading the same magazine page for the last two hours, as far as I can tell. Dominic returned Jacob and the "rescued" Director Bean to his employers this morning for debriefing.

All Sani and I can do now is wait. Wait for the president to make his move. Wait to see where the spinning wheel of public opinion lands. Wait to see if I'll end up a lauded hero or a hunted criminal. Wait to see if storm troopers bust down our door with tear gas and riot shields.

I hate waiting. I'd rather have the SWAT team.

I let out a loud sigh. "Isn't there anything else on? Cartoons?"

Sani picks up the remote control and simply turns off the TV. I'm not sure if the silence roaring from Marcy's corner is any better.

I trace the lines on Sani's palm in my lap. There are people who claim you can know anything you need to by looking at someone's palm, if you know what to look for. I'm not one of those people. I saw everything I needed to know on the roof today, Sani begging me to leave, knowing it would mean his death. And then again when I leaped after him, and he didn't doubt me for a second. Or two point two seconds.

Marcy hasn't spoken since we arrived at the hotel. So when she does now, I leap like a dreaming dog who's been rudely woken. "He did it for you, you know. For us."

I know she believes it. I know she needs to believe it. So I don't say anything even though I'm not convinced. Director Bean is one of the most secretive, manipulative humans in the known universe. He is the spy other spies study and aspire to be. I think he saw his main source of power yanked out from underneath him and made a desperate bid to take it back. A bid I upped the ante on by going all in. I am definitely not leaving my back unguarded until I figure out exactly what hand he's holding.

Nobody else says anything for several minutes. The air conditioner kicks on and whooshing air fills the silence. Marcy stands and retreats to her bedroom.

I'm melting into Sani's arms, drifting away from the thousands of thoughts wrestling for my attention when my cell phone rings. It's a miracle that thing's still working. I groan and snuggle farther into Sani's embrace, but he shifts underneath me, and the ringing gets closer.

"It could be important, Kitty," he says, pressing the phone into my palm.

I groan but answer the call in a singsong voice. "Kitty Lung, hero or terrorist, you take your pick."

"Thank you," the president's voice says, full of emotion. "I can never thank you enough for returning Jacob to me."

Despite the devil-may-care tone of my voice, I sit up straight, nerves taut as a violin string. "I gave you your family back. From where I'm sitting, the payback is pretty obvious." Sani's arms tighten around me, supporting and comforting me at the same time.

The president lets out a breath like a balloon plucked by a needle. "I can't release the dragons, Kitty."

A boulder rises up in my throat and, with considerable effort, I swallow it down. "You are the president of the United States. You can do whatever the hell you want."

"Popular misconception." He laughs sadly. "I am working on it, I promise. Director Bean has been helping me. But so far, the CIA is calling the shots on this one."

My brain screams at me: Liar! Liar! Liar! He lies so easily and so convincingly. I know I can't believe a word he says, but I want to.

I don't know what to say. Do I keep him as a friend or threaten him? Gods, I wish my mother were here. I've been quiet for too long. The president clears his throat, but I still don't respond.

"Give me some time," he says.

My dragon gives a little roar inside of me. Liquid steel runs through my veins. Maybe my mother is with me after all, in some way. "You know what I'm capable of, Mr. President. I will not wait forever."

I hang up and toss the phone across the room to land on a cushy armchair. Sani pulls me into his lap, cradling my head on his shoulder.

"How long will you wait?" he asks, pressing his lips to my temple.

A yawn tugs at my jaw and I give in to it. "First, I'm going to sleep for about a week."

His hot breath rushes across my skin as a soft laugh escapes his lips. I snuggle in closer to him, wrapping an arm around his stomach.

"And after the fierce dragon has had her catnap?"

Determination slides down my spine, stiffening my resolve. After everything, I'm not even entirely sure who's on my side anymore. I may not know the how, where, and when, but the "what" is the only thing that matters. "I'm getting my family back."

Acknowledgments

The first thanks goes to Chelsea Scheid, without whom this book would never exist — in many ways. Without you, my sky would have no sun. Eternal gratitude to Brenda Drake, who gave me the encouragement to keep going when I needed it most and for being one of the first to read this book! I have to say thanks to my dear, sweet Meg who gives me continuous encouragement and gave me a great critique of this book. Many thanks go to Jessica Souders who has helped me, cheered me on, and talked me down from several ledges. And what would I do without David Tiffany, who has proofread everything I've ever written and then buys it on release day, which messes up his Amazon recommendations! I'm so grateful to have my sister, Kayelee, to bounce ideas off of and to tell me when she thinks something's stupid — and to give me the sweetest, most perfect little niece this year! (I love you, Alice! You can read this in about 13 years!) Many thanks to mama and daddy, who have always worked so hard to give me and K everything we could ever need.

If I listed every person who's helped me along this journey, the acknowledgments would be longer than the book! Many thanks go to: Maurice Forrester, who was the first to suggest I write a full-length book; the past and current members of Yatopia and the YA Rebels; every member of every writing group I've ever been in, but especially Mike Taylor and Lisa Iriarte; everyone who's ever gone on a writing retreat with me; every agent and editor who provides free and plentiful advice, especially Colleen Lindsay, who taught me so much when I first started learning about the industry; every blogger and reader who has helped spread the word about this book, even before it came out; every teacher who never gave me a hard time about reading in the back of the class; and every single person who has encouraged or informed me in any way—you are not forgotten!

Much love to my agent, Rebecca Podos, for believing in this book and really getting Kitty, faults and all. I'm indebted to Terese for picking my book up and going to bat for it, and to Kate Brauning for giving it her all in edits! The entire team at Entangled is amazing and I'm so blessed to work with all of you.

About the Author

Sarah is a 30-something YA author who currently lives in Orlando with a 60-lb mutt who thinks he's a chihuahua. She believes that some boys are worth trusting, all girls have power, and dragons are people too.

She's a proud member of the Gator Nation and has a BS in Mechanical Engineering, but has switched careers entirely. She now works as an Event Coordinator for a County Library and as a freelance book publicist and author's assistant.

Find out more about her at www.sarahnicolas.com and check her out on Twitter @sarah_nicolas.

CPSIA information can be obtained at www.ICGtesting.com
Printed in the USA
BVOW06s1903230516

449219BV00016B/223/P